Absolutely Silly!

Tales from the North Pole.

Copyright ©Pete Shakespear 2017

All rights reserved. No part of this publication may be reproduced, stored in a retrieval system, or transmitted, in any form electronic, mechanical, photocopying, recording or otherwise, without the prior permission in writing of the author and publisher.

Please note: any reference to places and names mentioned in this story and any connections to persons now living or dead is purely coincidental.

This is a tale of fibs, fantasy, frolics and foolishness, lies, lunacy and laughter, toilet humour at its best, not one for the children! A totally irreverent peek at the ins and outs and ups and downs of Santa's world. Here we meet people from all over the Gnome world, a united nations of characters who let us enjoy a behind the scenes look at what may go on in a typical year at the North Pole workshop, and we learn......

There was once a Mrs Claus!

That each year Santa and his team make time trial runs across the night sky.

The North Pole is also subject to Elf and Safety.

There really is a pole at the centre of the North Pole?

What caused the biggest solar flare ever recorded? and much, much more through the silly and impossible situations Santa and his team find themselves in.

So, when the long winter nights are here, and there's nothing on the telly, or when you find you are getting under the wife's feet, or she is getting on top of you, curl up with Santa.

When the annual row about next summer's vacation is too early to begin, (will it be Spain or camping in Cornwall?) and the mother-in-law and wife's sisters are seeking new ways to question your parentage, and even the dog has gone off you, close the door and pour out your favourite tipple and escape to your comfy armchair. Sit down, relax and chuckle at the antics of: The Elves, The Tooth Fairy, The Firedrake and the Easter Bunny, all presided over by Rudolph and his mates, and of course ....

F. Christmas!

The Tales

Well, What a week, Who would keep reindeers?
6

Sod it, does nothing go right!
14

Do I really need a P.A.?
29

There used to be a Mrs Claus.
41

Enter Raymond.
50

George is not a Rodney.
66

Norman, Bloody Norman.
82

Shitzen, Santa's new reindeer.
99

Fish and Fleasels.
118

Pinkie it's Daddy.
130

Put that bloody light out.
140

Unto us a child is born.
151

Thieving little people and exploding pants!
165

Girder returns.
176

Pissards Electric Saloon.
189

Crew cut Sir?
197

Well, what a week!!! Who would keep reindeers?

Every year at the North Pole, before our departure around the world, we hold an open house party for all the staff and their families. This is a time of merriment and relaxation, and a way of saying thank you to all my loyal staff. This year's party had all started well, with plenty of bonhomie and promise.

Together we had enjoyed many glasses of mulled wine, eaten many hot mince pies, and seen off several flagons of Brandy to keep out the cold; and on this special night, everyone was in a merry mood. Rudolph was his usual self, showing off in front of the others and winking at the Elvelets. I've told them not to keep lifting their little skirts above their heads, as it puts impossible ideas in his mind. The naughty girls only continued to encourage him, as does the Tooth Fairy who keeps insisting on standing over mirrors. She would send the poor beast mad if I didn't stop her.

Rudolph was up to his annual trick of putting his red nose in the ears of younger reindeers and making it appear as if their ears were lit from the inside.

One or two of the inexperienced ones were panicked, and with a lot of snorting, sweating, and red veined bulging eyes, much expelling of air was heard, the foul emissions causing some older workers to faint. I will have to stop him being such a show off; he puts up this performance every year, although I'm sure that his behavior is getting worse. After a while and things calmed down, some vestige of order returned, and I was able to direct the Gnomes to bring round the reindeers and the sleigh, now fully loaded with presents. The team of my chosen reindeers, who have been with me for as long as I can remember, were harnessed together.

Rudolph, as is traditional, was leading from the front, and then came Dasher, Dancer, Prancer, Vixen, Comet, Cupid, Donner and Blitzen, they waited patiently, occasionally lifting a leg or snorting quietly and nodding knowingly to each other.

With the little helpers belted safely into the rear seat of the sleigh, all was now ready. I climbed aboard the sleigh, took the reins, 'Ho Ho hoed' and cracked my whip in the air. To the sound of great applause, back slapping and loud cheers from the little helpers and staff, we set off around the world.

We hadn't gone more than a few thousand miles when, being full of the Season's spirit and the cold air mixing with the Brandy, I began to feel a little light headed. Failing to negotiate a landing properly, I caught the backside of my new red pants on a television aerial, almost impaling myself in the process.

With my flailing arms trying to remove the spikes out of my nether regions, I lurched violently, and in a vain attempt to attain to freeness, I slipped and plunged head first into the chimney. Suddenly I felt the rush of cold winter air in a place I hadn't felt it before. The chortling and smirking from the reindeers and Elves alerted me to the fact that something was amiss!

I knew that I had put on a little weight since last year but I was stuck fast, the more I struggled the more I was forced deeper into the chimney, like a cork in a bottle. All my past flashed before me, oh why did I decide to keep reindeers, at least monkeys could have been trained to have the sense to know that something was wrong and come to my aid, but they were no help, they just watched me making a fool of myself. I now know how the trainees must have felt at the antics of that show off Rudolph.

With much leg twisting and thrusting, after what appeared to be an age, I finally extricated myself. It was then that I realised that all had gone quiet, the sleigh, along with its contents, reindeers and crew had gone. The Elves, little buggers, had taken the opportunity during my predicament, to take control of the reins and talk the silly bloody animals into going to a party. Leaving me without transport I had to walk back to the North Pole through the Earth's upper atmosphere. To stop the terrible draught in my trousers, I stuffed one of my gloves into the torn hole made by the aerial. On returning to the workshop I was informed of the panic that had ensued as I was seen silhouetted against the Northern sky; the Nit Nurse and Harold the Doctor, our medical team, were rushed out and assumed that due to the cold, I had developed an udder! I spent hours on the telephone arranging emergency help from my department store colleagues all over the world. We made it, but only just! I didn't sleep at all well that night

The Elves and reindeers returned several days later without the sleigh, looking guilt ridden. They are now in disgrace and all on written warnings. From the story now slowly emerging, they apparently stopped somewhere near a village in the Urals and stole some home brewed Vodka, kidding themselves that it was only potato lemonade. From the look of them, it appears they have been on a 'bender.'

I don't know how, but somewhere on their travels they had collected items of female underwear and on their return were seen swinging them triumphantly in the air. The garments were sack-like in texture, long legged with reinforced gussets, strangely of natural colour, of a folk design, and of a larger size. They tried to placate my anger by claiming that they would be useful for storing winter vegetables or as nosebags to hold feed for the livestock, but I was having nothing to do with it. I didn't want my animals possibly poisoned or any strange odours on my comestibles, and so immediately I ordered the fearsome things destroyed.

Fortunately they burned ferociously, even if they were a little smoky, and they kept the workshop fire alight for days.

Thankfully the sleigh was finally found, although not surprisingly minus the presents. It was reported by a passing airline pilot after he spotted it abandoned on a peak in the Pyrenees mountain range. I don't know where on earth the presents went, but I'm guessing the Elves did a deal with some intergalactic market traders and flogged them off cheap. Nobody will own up to what happened, nor to taking the jingle out of the bells or even writing rude words about me in the snow, or letting on how they managed to write them, but I have my suspicions.

We picked up the message of the sleigh sighting in our North Pole radio shack as the pilot excitedly reported the find to air traffic control. On the air traffic controllers instructions the pilot was ordered to land at the nearest airport, whereupon he was immediately arrested, and threatened with the sack if he ever spoke about what he had seen, which is good for us I suppose. Norman, our Gnome chief mechanic and his team were dispatched poste-haste to collect the sleigh.

To my dismay I now find that Rudolf has taken a shine to the illicit Vodka. It should have been destroyed, but unfortunately someone had brought back a few bottles and kept it as a secret stash, until it was discovered in the medical room disguised as cough mixture. It was only after the Nit Nurse prescribed the liquid to a chesty Gnome that, after several days on the stuff, he became afraid to cough. He appeared at the medical room with both hands clasping his bottom to hold his cheeks together and walking in a strange manner, croaking that his chest felt like it was on fire, and his stomach was out of sorts.

Rudolph now sits alone on a bench in the Animal Park clutching a bottle of the foul liquid. It's wrapped in a brown paper bag, and he keeps holding it to his cheek and talking to it. He thinks I don't know what he is doing, but I'm not the only one who has noticed his eyes are glassy and he constantly slides off the bench. I've tried to take the bag away from him but he gets narked and spits at me. He is now beginning to smell a bit. He hasn't cleaned his teeth or changed his antlers for several days, dirty boy, but thankfully he has lost all interest in the Elvelets and the Tooth Fairy. His nose is slowly turning purple, and he is mumbling a lot about being overworked and nobody understanding him, and something about me not letting him have a hobby. It will be a couple of days before the Goblins come to collect him and take him into rehab, so I will leave him alone until then.

I've just picked up my red trousers from the cleaners; apparently, soot is one of the most difficult things to get out of fabric, and the robbing buggers charged me forty pounds for invisible mending!! I can't see it! What a rip off!! Bah humbug! If it keeps on like this I'm going to retire.

This year has been a total wash out.

I'm beginning to lose belief in myself.

Sod it, does nothing go right!

After a struggle, we finally managed to get Rudolph into rehab. It happened like this......

It was a cold, frosty, starry night. We were working late at the office when we noticed him spread eagled by the bench in the park that had become his resting place and bed for the last few weeks. Harold the North Pole Doctor, armed with a syringe filled with his own mixture of unknown medicine, took along a couple of the larger Gnomes and crept up on Rudolph. Harold, his face glowing red, his eyes having a strange concentrated stare and his hands trembling slightly with excitement, jabbed Rudolph triumphantly several times with the needle, 'drunken bastard' he kept hissing, 'drunken bastard,' until the Gnomes pulled him off, still grabbing and punching and his arms flailing. He was gurgling and cackling, but eventually after a struggle, they got him away from the poor animal. The Gnomes then threw a cargo net around Rudolph just as he began to realise what was happening, I must confess I've never heard such language from a reindeer, I know that I had a grandfather so the rest must be a lie!

Within minutes a team of white coated Goblins arrived in a cigar shaped flying saucer. Rudolph was quickly loaded into the machine and dispatched from the North Pole.

He had been booked into a rehab clinic in Switzerland run by someone I had known for years, Dr Goandbollo. We had selected this location because we felt that the cold mountain air would help Rudolph feel more at home.

Goandbollo's methods are somewhat unorthodox, the cure for all ailments apparently always being the same. The doctor prescribes for his patients partly rest, and partly a diet of syrup of figs and liquid paraffin. The good doctor firmly believing that, 'a good purging' will cure anything. He also encourages communal intercourse with the other residents. As I write, and for the moment, Rudolph is quite happy and settled there. He is getting along well with the other patients and has made friends with several well known show business people including someone named Boyle, who told him that they started life as a little pimple! I've told him not to believe all he hears. He seems happy regaling to the others tales and exploits of his life, but it's sad that nobody really takes him seriously; perhaps it's just as well.

The Elves have been on extra good behaviour, no bickering or back chat for days, they are feeling guilty about the trouble they have caused no doubt. I've put them to work making silver new nothings, so that will keep them quiet for a while.

Now that the sleigh is back, Norman our chief mechanic is repairing it and fashioning new dingily bits for the jingle bells, and getting it ready for use later on in the year. At the moment all appears to be in harmony. I can hear him humming quietly to himself as he works away, ah.

It's been a month now since Rudolph's internment, he comes back next week so we have arranged to collect him and organized a little get-together with the Easter Bunny, the Fire Drake and the Tooth Fairy, but the whole of the team are excited and want to contribute to the party, which I feel is nice.

The Easter Bunny is quite a strange lad. Around March each year he begins jumping up and down a lot in an excited manner as if he were expecting something. He later disappears, only to reappear after about a month with wobbly legs and looking pale and tired, I don't know what on earth he gets up to but the Elvelets seem to like him and other than that he is no harm.

The noisy old Fire Drake on the other hand can be a nuisance. He came to us from a county in England, appearing one night during a thunderstorm. He said he had got lost, but has stayed ever since. He can be a bad tempered old buggar, constantly leaping through the lit logs in the fireplace of the workshop. It would be madness to allow him into my private quarters as I keep a fire constantly burning in the grate, and with my nerves in the state they are I'm sure to end up in the same place as poor Rudolph.

He seems to derive great pleasure in hiding in the logs until the fire is lit, and when a good 'blizzy' is going he pokes his long neck out through the flames and honks toward the unsuspecting and relaxing soul, usually just as they are about to warm their hands by the fire, or rub butter into a little crumpet. (There's been many occasion when I have had to take an Elvelet into my private quarters and comfort her.) I told him that he was a naughty boy and that he should stop this immature behaviour. He said he hadn't had much work since the introduction of boiler central heating and was a bit bored, and had nowhere to play. I felt a bit sorry for him really, but I didn't like his fascination with fire, hmmm, better watch him!

The Tooth Fairy has been around the workshop for as long as I can remember. She is usually to be found in the packing department, but she will move around a bit and do other favours if asked nicely. She has a large gap at the front of her multi-coloured collection of teeth that causes her to whistle and lisp when she speaks. (In fact it is said by the Elves that if she had a white tooth she would have a snooker set.) Her appearance and voice remind one somewhat of the late Marilyn Munroe.

Excitement rose in the North Pole as the day drew

nearer for Rudolph to come home. At last, with Rudolph on board, our small communications flying saucer that we keep here at the North Pole and which had been dispatched that morning to collect him, came into sight, just as dusk was falling. The Northern lights were switched on as a special welcome for our returning hero and a small oompah band played merrily in the sleigh park. A floodlit barbeque was started by the mechanics and the Goblins arranged for a bouncy castle to be inflated in the workshop. Rudolph's stable had been washed and polished by the Elves and the Gnomes, and with a new carpet of fresh straw it looked fit for a king. I do hope he likes it.

Although bigger than Elves and quite gruff, Gnomes do have a softer side, and they have shown it by decorating Rudolf's quarters with pin up pictures of the Elvelets, along with bunting and flags made from old work clothes. I only hope the pictures do not have an adverse effect on Rudolph after Goandbollo's treatment and hard work.

Rudolph was recovering quietly in his stable, when late one afternoon the Elves decided to do him a nicety to make him feel better, by changing the red bulb in his nose. This seemingly small act of kindness unfortunately was to trigger a chain of events that may possibly take months to recover from, and for the workshop production team to get back to the position they were in before the fracas.

As part of our pattern of life, after our Christmas night travels, here at the Pole we have an annual little rest, a few days off from our labours, it's a chance to recharge our batteries. During the break I caught up on some darning of socks, sewing on shirt buttons and other chores about my quarters which made it a bit more pleasant to come home to, including plumbing in a new welly washing machine. As you can imagine, with all the livestock around, the pungent straw lodges in the tracks of my boots and I am constantly having to scrape it off the bedclothes, my candlewick is particularly difficult to keep clean and at times can become smelly!

After our break we had returned to work early in the New Year with renewed gusto and had begun the season with the production of a new range of children's toys. We were getting along quite well in the dolls, prams and teddy bears section, and had quickly built up a stockpile of newly modelled dollies and these were being made ready to be put into the stores awaiting our annual sleigh ride later in the year. The specially designed packaging for them had arrived from the print room and the Tooth Fairy and her team were busy making the dollies presentable in their brightly coloured see-through boxes.

Nearby in a corner of the workshop, the Elves had set up an aluminium ladder borrowed from our mean spirited storekeeper, Bert. This in itself was unusual, as Bert allows nothing out of the stores, and makes long winded heavy work of every request, considering that all items in the stores belong to him. On this occasion though he appeared to be in a mellow mood and let them have the ladders without complaint or question.

This is unusual as I said, because Bert has a reputation for meanness that is beyond belief and is rumoured to be able to peel an orange with one hand in his pocket! but I felt that perhaps Bert was turning over a new leaf and settling down, and I determined to make a note of this in his file for when the annual staff appraisals were held.

I watched quietly from a distance as the Elves gently brought Rudolph into the workshop from his stable, and settled him down. One of them climbed the ladder. With Rudolph now standing in position, a little worker Elf in a blue safety hat and standing on top of the ladder was holding the new bulb, the other Elf, a supervisor, was looking up at him and giving orders, holding a screwdriver and appearing very managerial. The Elf carefully began to twist and pull at the reindeer's nose. Rudolph stood there patiently. Off came the red cover.

Into Rudolph's nose he began to screw the new bulb. On changing the bulb, the little fools had inadvertently tried to insert the wrong recommended wattage, causing Rudolph's left eye to fuse, sending sparks flying from every orifice and limb ending. This panicked the poor creature so much that a stream of offensive smelly brown liquid ejected forcefully from the rear end of Rudolph and up the workshop wall, covering the new dollies that had been made for the forthcoming winter season. He bolted, but his fear was such that he left a trail of liquid and debris that soon led us to where he had hidden himself. I don't know what the substance was, but I guess that it was residue from the stolen Vodka! I suppose it had to come out sometime, perhaps Dr Goandbollo hadn't purged Rudolph quite enough. It all ended up in a bit of a mess. The workshop wall will definitely need re-painting and if we work hard, we might possibly save some of the stock.

After a bad tempered production and marketing meeting, we have decided to re-name the dollies from what we thought could be a world winner of 'New York Lady Who Lunches' complete with spray on orange tan, to a now more realistic 'Eastern European Farm Hand Girl' complete with farmers brown hands. We may be able to save some of the packaging as well, if it doesn't stain and wrinkle too much when it dries out, although it's not see-through any more. Perhaps we will try wrapping the dollies in straw to make them more appealing and rustic.

I've put a team of Elves to clearing up the mess,

they are working away quietly, but I can hear them grumbling under their breath. Unfortunately, due to Elf and Safety I have had to dismiss the two Elves responsible for the upset, but I hear that they have found employment at Woolworths; I hope the pair will behave themselves for their new employer, and have a long career with the company. If we push hard we should recover production schedules and hopefully the next few months will see us back on target. In the meantime I have other work to do.

I have been asked to evaluate several books sent to me by the publishers, some of which I am really looking forward to reading.

From the Self Improvement section: 'No Qualifications? Self Belief Will Advance Your Career,' this looks like a book written by a politician.

'The Successful Grumbler,' this should be good for Bert. From the Health and Fitness section I'm sure I could benefit from 'Tap Dance Your Way to a Regular Bowel Movement' and 'Cure Constipation' by E.Z. Turder.

'You and Your Penis,' by Dr Tosser should be

enlightening. From the Human Relationships section come several interesting titles: 'Let's Stop Avoiding Each Other-We Both Have Halitosis.' And: 'Flatulence Can Be Beaten, Make It Your Friend.' But, 'Annoying Nail Biting? Stop using toilet paper!' I don't know, this book doesn't seem very appetizing.

I am particularly looking forward to reading, 'My Years in Russian Striptease,' an autobiography by Flipma Tittyup.

To set the mood, I will place my favourite record on the old Dansette which was presented to me at finishing school. The graduation ceremony was wonderful, the citation on my prize read, 'To the Santa most likely to succeed.'

I will make a mug of hot chocolate and lock the office door and settle down to work, soothed by the wonderful tones of The Gnomettes and their silky lead singer Nat King Gnome:

*We are the Gnomes and we can help you, magic we can provide, Sparkle in children's eyes, down on a dream you'll slide,
If you've a tear then we can change it into a happy smile,
Crying is not the style with Santa.
In a rainbow, through a moonbeam where Santa Claus resides,*

Ice cream fountains, Sugar Mountains, Toadstools side by side, From dust till dawn you'll see us working, Never to complain, Sunny Sundays, Misty Mondays Singing in the rain.

*So if you've a tear then we can change it into a happy smile,
Crying is not the style with Santa.*

©Pete Shakespear & Pat Hannon

My review of Flipma's autobiography was most enlightening. I can only say that this is one of the finest exposés of Russian nightlife that I have ever read. I admit that the book is not for the faint hearted as it contains several photographs taken of her at the end of her career, when she modelled for The Moscow Novelty Balloon Company, but it's informative and entertaining nonetheless, although not in a medical sense. I feel that had she had more guidance and allowed herself to be manipulated more, this woman could have become a big star.

Goodness! What on earth is that noise, there's something happening in the workshop.

Sod it! Does nothing go right!!

Just as I'm relaxing something happens. I had better go and see what's going on......

Those silly little Elves are shouting and jumping about like crickets, whooping and punching the air.

What on earth are they up to? Oh, No!!

They have talked the Tooth Fairy into performing a pole dance, and she is silly enough to try as well!!! The little fool! There's quite a crowd gathering and somebody is spraying water on her vest! She looks like she has developed a couple of boils! I must go in and stop them!!!

'Pack it up! Stop!!

You dirty girl, cover yourself up!!

Get back to work all of you! Stop I say!

Someone get me a hacksaw!!'

The silly girl's got herself twisted all shapes, and the boils are getting bigger, we may have to send for Harold!

The Elves are still cheering. They think that I've joined in with the pole dance. They are now spraying me with water.

'Stop it!' 'Stop it; you're making the red dye run on my costume!'

I can't stand much more, I will retire, I can feel it!!

Do I really need a P.A.?

With a struggle I managed to take down the pole, and finally succeeded in sawing it up into smaller lengths, ensuring that it couldn't be used again for such a questionable purpose. Although, I've noticed several of the Elveletes quietly taking a piece, I suspect they want it for firewood.

I had noticed that the stress of dealing with all my duties and coping with the Elves naughtiness was, of late, getting to me and making me a little bad tempered. So I decided to place an advert in 'Seasons Greetings' magazine for a personal assistant. The journal is distributed throughout the Gnome world.

Within a few days of the magazine being published I received several sacks of letters in answer to the advertisement. I was still feeling tense and worked up but after taking the Tooth Fairy into my private quarters, putting her across my knee and giving her a good spanking, the naughty girl was by now feeling thoroughly chastised and I was feeling better.

After we both got our breath back, we began to

sift through the applications and make a shortlist of possible prospects. We had in mind someone who would be able to fit in with the team and be able to take on the job of organising all the departments, helping them to achieve maximum efficiency.

Interviews were scheduled for a Friday. We prepared a list of questions and attributes that we were looking for in the ideal candidate, and a job specification that would cover all likely duties expected from the new employee.

We particularly enjoyed the application from a Gnome that to date had had quite an interesting career, and along with other likely candidates, we invited him along to an interview. A 'Do Not Disturb' notice was placed on the door handle to my office, and a couple of dried toadstools which we use as chairs were arranged around a table. On the table we placed a selection of fairy cakes and pots of tea and coffee.

A knock was heard on my office door, 'Come In, ith's open,' the Tooth Fairy shouted. As he entered the room, the candidate's appearance told us immediately that he was from a spicy hot land. He was one of our

Gnome colleagues who had graduated from the giftware manufacturing sector of that nation. He had a sparkle in his right eye; the left eye was covered with a bright red eye patch made from silk material. He smiled freely, revealing several gold teeth.

The gentleman sat awkwardly on a toadstool at the table with me and the Tooth Fairy, and we asked him if he would like tea or coffee to help him relax. It should be noted at this point that my skills as an interviewer are not particularly sharp, but when he requested a large scotch on the rocks I was shocked, nevertheless we continued with the interview.

It transpired that this man was now living in England, in a town that used to manufacture leather goods, and in his letter he explained that this would prove to be common ground due to the fact that I had 'livestock!' and he understood leather harnesses and business practice.

'Thank you for coming, tell us a little about yourself.'

'Are merte, ow are ya? I'm from the Midlands in England aye eye.'

'What is your background?' I asked, still believing it was going to be OK.

'Well I used to ab a market stall sellin' leder glubs an' stuff. Are med um all meself, yo no, glubs, 'ats, leder jackits, but there wore no demand an' I went bust day eye.'

'I see.'

'Ar but since then I bin karaoke singin' aye eye.'

'Oh yeth,' said the Tooth Fairy, obviously enthralled by the man's accent, 'And under whath name do you perform?'

'Gerupta Sing.'

'What!!' We both gasped!

'How thid you come to have a pathch on one eye?' she continued.

He raised his hands and gripped his head.

'Well, I like a drink when I sing doe eye, an are wuz cummin ome from a gig abart two in the mornin' when I slipped off the kerb artside me owse,

I slip, ...

Pavement comes up ....

Fall on eye ....

Eyelash break ....

Crack eye ....

Eye bulge ....

Bulge gets big ....

I scream ....

I bounce ....'

It was then I stepped in and said, 'Get out man; you're making a fool of yourself!'

After sipping a glass of cold water he was removed from the premises quietly and quickly.

Although feeling a little upset, we decided to continue with the interviews.

'Who is next?' I asked the Tooth Fairy.

'The nextht one I've chothen is a professthional manager.' 'Ooh sounds good,' I said, 'let's get him in.'

Into the room came a greying and balding older Goblin. He shook my hand firmly, and confidently assured us that he was what you call, 'a professional manager' and that I had probably noticed that from his C.V.

This meant, he went on to explain, that he could manage any project he was given, was computer literate and fully aware of company law.

He understood 'Maslow's Hierarchy of Needs' and felt confident that production would rise immeasurably under his leadership and guiding influence. We sent him to the canteen so we could discuss his application. The Tooth Fairy seemed impressed, but I explained that I had seen 'his sort' of manager before. I felt he might be a little too overconfident and may upset the applecart by jumping in and throwing his weight about. It had taken a long time to get the workforce to understand the yearly cycles and prove their willingness to rise to the occasion when called for. A common trick for this sort of operator was to join a company and immediately sack a prominent member of staff to establish their authority, and show others how hard they were going to be. This kind of weak manager loved the title 'hatchet man,' until of course, someone did it to them. I felt uneasy, and on recalling him from the canteen, told him so. I said that we couldn't see him fitting in, and sent him on his way.

So much for 'hatchet man'. The Goblin burst into

tears, he had been unemployed for at least a year. I wonder why? (We later learned that in his last post he had secured a position at a well known firm which made the sign posts for the motorways and sky highways, including the place names of towns, cities and places of interest. Unfortunately, in his haste to show off, 'hatchet man' had inadvertently failed to check his directions properly and stupidly had the signs manufactured backwards and pointing in the wrong direction. This caused universal chaos and cost the company its business; eventually the whole workforce lost their jobs.) Close call or what? A couple of months later, after we found out about the heartache that he had caused, the Tooth Fairy thanked me appropriately for my insight.

During the morning we had a succession of so called experts through the office, including a man who had been taken on by the largest training organisation in the world; his previous job was working for a credit card company. His speciality was 'lateral thinking.'

Another whiz kid had been managing a small company supplying toilet rolls, janitorial and rubber goods to industry. His previous background had been selling pens and pencils, his main client then being a chain of booksellers and office stationers. He proudly informed us that his speciality was a development of his own, **S**elected **H**igh **I**ntensity **T**raining. Needless to say, none of these companies were still trading.

By now, as the last of the morning's hopefuls set out his stall, we longed for the lunch break. Setting up an overhead projector he impressed us with graphs and ratios and even gave us a 'handout,' for us to keep. He informed us that his 'management style' was one of firm but fair, but wouldn't stand to be messed about. He believed fervently in lists, and checking every movement of the staff, also assuring us that, 'He wasn't a corporate tosser', and knew what to do and 'he was our man.' He said that he was known as, 'Mr Fix it.'

Feeling tired and unimpressed, I am afraid that I angrily retorted, 'Nothings broken,' and I asked him to leave. The Tooth Fairy helped him with his tackle and escorted him off the premises.

Over a subdued lunch in the works canteen, we discussed our disappointment, and wondered if we would ever find the right person for the post. Reluctantly, and with a heavy heart, the Tooth Fairy and I returned to the office to face the afternoon ahead.

Knock, knock, knock!

'Come in.'

Girder entered the room.

Girder was a well built, perhaps even husky German girl, looking suspiciously like Desperate Dan, but with pigtails. She had strong arms, as if she had been a shot putter or some other sort of athlete, a weight lifter perhaps. She pulled up a dried toadstool and sat down heavily. She suddenly smiled!

'What are your hobbies?' I asked. Her reply was revealing. To keep the cheeks of her gluteus-maximus strong she enjoyed cracking walnuts between them. As she spoke she rolled the muscles in her stomach and explained that pelvic floor exercises made for a healthy body, a healthy mind, and a happy marriage, her face flushed a little as she fidgeted on the toads tool. She boasted that she could, with a little more practise, at five metres, shoot ping pong balls into a bucket. It was when she tried to explain from where she fired the balls, and how she stored them that the Tooth Fairy fainted; I must confess I did get a little hot myself. She appeared well mannered, if slightly shy.

I asked her what she could bring to the post. She explained that she was typically German and highly efficient, and could help with not only running the workshop, but was prepared to act as my au-pair, everything from cooking, washing my clothes and keeping the wood store tidy. She was quite happy dealing with enquiries and giving orders. I sent her to the canteen for a sausage roll, and after discussing her application with the Tooth Fairy, who by now was a little jealous, I decided to give her a three month trial.

This arrangement proved altogether quite a blessing. Among other things I now had the time to read my letters. I get sacks full of mail each year around autumn, sent to me by children from all over the world. I had more time to help with the design of new toys, and had time to spend on my hobby, collecting and swapping photographs of reindeers.

Girder developed many friendships in her first few weeks with us. Many a morning I heard her shouting across the workshop, 'Rous' and 'Shizenhausen' to several of the Elvelets who happened to be in earshot, although I haven't found out who 'Dummkopf' is yet.

One evening, I returned to my quarters after a long day in the snowfields taking photographs of my favourite reindeer subjects. I was feeling quite relaxed. As I entered the door, Girder welcomed me home. 'Ah Fhader, mein hero,' she gushed. Putting down the orange plastic basket, which was full of washing that she had just finished wringing out with her hands, she ushered me to the table. There was a strange glint in her eye.

Girder had made a wonderful dinner of roast venison, mashed potato and sauerkraut. There was a marching tune playing pompously on the Dansette. She had cracked a few walnuts for afters, and I settled down to enjoy the evening.

I had just finished the last mouthful of sauerkraut, and was brushing breadcrumbs from my beard, when she began to loom toward me, pigtails flying, her ample bosom almost snapping my spectacles. I felt the throb of her biceps around by body, and the thrust of a large nipple made me go deaf in one ear.

'Oh Fhader Christmas, you vunderbar man, what a trick!'

I must confess it shook me, I realised that I may be trapped, but the look of terror in my eyes must have brought Girder to her senses.

'What trick?' I screamed!

Laughingly she said, 'No, I mean you are clever man, I do washing today and I know you smoke, but no one see, only I.'

'Smoke,' I said confused, 'Santa doesn't smoke!'

'Yes, you smoke through bottom,' she said proudly.

'You smoke through bottom; I see nicotine stains on pants.'

She was gone within the hour. I hoped that she had not spread this news to the other members of staff.

Do I really need a P.A.?

It will be several months before we pluck up the courage to re-advertise the position, oh dear!

There used to be a Mrs Claus

Not many people know this, but yes, there used to be a Mrs Claus. We met when I was a young trainee in New York. I had just been posted there from finishing school in Northern Lapland. I was putting on weight nicely and had learned to 'Ho, Ho, Ho' like an old pro. I had received a thorough education in a town called Myra, from where it is rumoured our ancestors came. A legend grew up around some of my family members which say's they gave small gifts to strangers.

It is funny, that even in the modern age, people still really believe in the legend, but if it makes them happy then I don't stop them, most humans find out soon enough.

I must confess that I don't make all the toys myself now, you can't get the labour, and most 'little people' prefer to try their hand at being film extras. No, I have to rely on the Chinese and Indian manufacturing sector to produce the quantity of toys I need. We do our best to keep up at the North Pole, but there are so many chimneys and people to deliver presents to, that it makes it harder each year to keep up with demand. But I do enjoy the annual sleigh ride.

I recall many happy memories. I remember once delivering a couple of books to a President who had just taken over from his father. I can't remember his name. Sadly the books were later stolen, and the poor President hadn't finished crayoning them in.

I wonder if a female prime minister ever read the book I delivered, 'Kindness and Compassion.' It's strange the things you remember.

Over the years some of the family moved to other parts of the world including Holland and Germany where they set up their own workshops, but now they have disappeared. In the early nineteenth century we transferred the main operation to America, and had a change of costume; someone seemed to think that dressing our family like Mr Sinterklaas, a Dutchman, would help people get along better. It was when, Queen Victoria of England married a German Prince, that most of the traditions associated with our family developed, and of course some of the great commercial empires were born. Around 1930 the full costume was designed, and has remained pretty well the same ever since. I was following in a long line of Santa's and wanted the family to be proud of me.

Time has moved on, and sadly I am now the last of the line, so when I retire there will be no more to carry on the tradition; unless I produce offspring with the Tooth Fairy. The chances of that are slim, as my age is now against me, and I must confess that after a day at the workshop, rather than good old rumpy pumpy I prefer a good bacon sandwich! Although I confess to living in hope after reading a letter in the agony aunt column of the local newspaper. It was from a gentleman who wrote:-

'*Dear Agony Aunt,*

When I was 18 I could grasp my penis with both hands but could not bend it. I am now 85 and can still grasp my penis with both hands and can now bend it a little. Does this mean that I am getting stronger?'

Anyway, modern people seem ok to be missing the importance of the season, most have become consumer focused and have little time for the simple things in life.

When I met Mrs Claus at the opening of a toy shop in New York all those years ago, she was a stripling of a thing, no more than fourteen stones or so. She told me she was a kick starter of jet engines at JFK Airport. Oh those thighs! Her family was part Dutch and part German. She had heard of my family, and was eager to catch up with the past history and write home that she had met me.

She insisted on being called 'Claus.' I invited 'Claus' to a mud wrestling match. It was during the second bout that we fell in love, I think that the sight of those rubbery, sticky, shiny, sweating bodies, wallowing about in filth, excited her. We were married the next day at a small holiday motel in Las Vegas, to the sounds of a Gospel choir singing 'White Christmas.'

The home we set up together was a small log cabin in the Yukon. She had furnished it with pictures of her family back home in Europe and Seattle, and some old friends from her days in show business when she worked for a while in England. There, she was re-writing scripts for speech impaired ventriloquists with regional accents and who used offensive language. She found herself out of work when this type of comedy suddenly became new and alternative; speech correction was no longer required. Whilst between jobs she had taken a position with a troupe of acrobats working their passages back to America,. She had had it hard.

We were blissfully happy. She would make my favourite meal, shepherd's pie, until someone rumbled that shepherds were disappearing at an alarming rate from Tibetan villages. Happily for me, the locals blamed the Bigfoot and Yeti working together. We would make love for hours on a specially imported bed made in Europe. We saw it advertised in 'Mud Mania,' the monthly magazine we subscribed to. As a gesture of goodwill, and to spread a little happiness, we decided to give away the extra rubber free gifts which were offered with the bed, to a local religious order; how they seemed to appreciate them. To help them with finding new members they formed a friendship circle.

During my study evenings, 'Claus' would ask me questions from the Civil Aviation Authority Code of

Practise Manual, to ensure that I knew the air traffic routes to avoid on my annual journey across the sky. She would test me out with highly complex astronomical, meteorological and social problems such as, 'Where is Uranus situated?' 'How would I handle wind in the Trossachs?' and, 'What would I do if caught by the Peelers or felt the beat of a Policeman's truncheon?'

All went well for several years until, as the business grew, I had to spend more time away from the cabin, looking for new premises and staff at the North Pole. Whilst I was away, I think she began to long for something more, perhaps something larger than I was able to provide; something bigger than I had to offer.

Our neighbours, the Snotballers, a family of Gold prospectors who had lived in the Yukon for many years, wrote me to say that she had not been seen for weeks at the cabin; they thought she had gone back to her mother. I sent letters expressing my undying love, and presents of snow globes, and then slowly, she eventually began to come around to the idea of a fresh start.

In a letter to her mother, Zena, I assured her that I did have a birth certificate and I wasn't hatched and that it was not part of me up the alley wall. Her mother said she didn't know what 'Claus' saw in me in the first place, I was a has-been with no future, and that her daughter had thrown away the best years of her life on me, and if her father was alive, he would have had something to say about this. But bit by bit our relationship began to thaw. 'Claus' eventually joined me at the workshop, but things were not the same.

She began to isolate herself, spending hours reading. Her favourite book was 'Scouting for Boys,' by a man named Powell. I don't know why, but one evening, on entering her room to offer her some hot cocoa, I found the book partly torn up and partly burning in the fireplace. She had a sad, disappointed look on her face.

Late one evening, to cheer her up, I asked her to accompany me and a couple of Elves on a time test flight on the routes I had planned for later in the season. (As you can imagine, we have to do this, what with the growing number of housing estates, people, and air traffic, the journey gets a little longer each year, and I have to ensure that I cover all the territory in the same night.)

It was somewhere over Southern England that she spotted a man down at the bottom of his garden, playing with his telescope. I noticed that she could not take her eyes off the scene below.

On the way back to the North Pole she became quiet and reflective. My guess is that she imagined she saw something in him. For a couple of weeks afterwards she enjoyed baking, well, not so much the baking, but rolling the dough into fat, long, sausage-like things. Her eyes and thoughts were elsewhere, far away from the North Pole.

How she caressed that dough; she had the cleanest hands I ever saw during those troubled times. I also remember we had a lot of misshapen French sticks during those weeks and it also appeared that she had been attempting to make cobs!

I awoke one morning early, to find that during the night she had packed a few skimpy things into a case, and gone! I later found several of the larger French sticks still under her bed.

By the time I had dressed, most of the workshop had heard the news; the Tooth Fairy said that she had been expecting it for a while now.

The note found on the kitchen mantelpiece behind the clock read:

'Santa's personal guarantee of satisfaction is not worth the paper it is written on.'

I don't eat bread much now.

Enter Raymond

Everyone at the workshop saw my sadness; this sort of news gets out very quickly. There are some days when I miss Girder, gargling 'the happy wanderer' in a morning, the crack of walnut shells in the evening, even the occasional sound of a ping pong ball in the bottom of a bucket. It's no secret that her home made pumpernickel bread did bind me a little, but now my morning looseness brings a tinge of sadness; but I am walking better and I am now able to straighten my back more. My quarters sadly seem roomy and quiet. I still keep her lederhosen hanging off the corner of the headboard of my bed as a constant reminder of her perfume.

It may have been my demeanour that gave me away, or the fact that dirty dishes were beginning to stack up in the sink and I had no clean socks or underwear, and flies were beginning to follow me about, whatever it was, I found myself the talk of the factory, and the local watering hole, Pissards Electric Saloon. (I will tell you more about the goings on at this place later). Suffice to say that I stood no chance of privacy, what with the barmaid Sarah being such a nosey parker, always pumping anyone she could, and wanting to know everyone's business. She doesn't get out much so she feeds on the woes of others. What made it harder to keep things quiet was her father and husband both worked in the factory in the cleaning department, and they all spent a lot of time together. They were all equally as nosey.

Some of the Elvelets had put little chocolate sweets outside my office door with touching notes saying they loved me. This kind gesture made me feel better. The Tooth Fairy said that I must not dwell on my problem and I would soon find someone else, and she promised to take me in hand and help me to forget.

That day, the sky in the North Pole was a bright azure blue, the rising sun low in the northern sky, it's rays reflecting on the snow like sparkling diamonds, turning my fancy to other things. The Tooth Fairy had given of her services and cleared the washing up. I had taken a long soak in the bath and the washing machine was whirring quietly in the kitchen. With a new sense of purpose I decided to pull myself together. I did my usual morning's rounds visiting the workshop departments with a spring in my step.

After some light refreshment in my private quarters with the Tooth Fairy, I decided to re-advertise the position for a helper for me. I soon felt relieved, things were on the up. Word had got out around the workshop that I was indeed seeking an assistant, and several members of the staff approached me throughout the afternoon requesting an interview. One such person was the Fire Drake, who telephoned after lunch to see if I was in, and could I see him immediately. When I agreed, he flew across the yard and was let in the window by the Tooth Fairy.

The Fire Drake tried very hard to convince me that his behaviour would improve if he had more responsibility, but at the sight of the flame from the match that the tooth Fairy used to light her slim Cuban panatela (she always enjoyed one in the afternoon) he pounced! 'Hhhhaaarnnnkkk!!' he hissed, his long neck sent his beak hurtling toward the poor maiden. As he lunged, I just managed to clip him on the side of his angry face with the cigar box, but not before the panatela was half way down his throat! He gasped, the air in the office now had a smell of singed feathers and burning beak and he began to emit steam from his nostrils. One wing clutched his throat. The other wing tried violently to maintain lift and stable flight, as he clumsily exited the open window. The Tooth Fairy, now reduced to a flood of tears, sank to her knees. It took me several hours to comfort the poor girl and bring a smile to her face once again.

The witless bird has sat dejectedly in a corner of the workshop unable to honk, much to the relief of all. Later I went over to see if he was recovering. He croaked to me an apology, saying he felt a little silly and that soon, any day now, he hoped he would be able to pass the panatela. I told him that it would have to be at his own convenience as these things cannot be a rushed affair.

Subsequently, I was stopped on the garage forecourt by Norman our chief mechanic, who had also got the idea that he would be my number one choice to take over the running of the workshop.

'Got a minute guv?' he smiled; wiping oil from his hands with an old rag. I guessed what it was about. I immediately felt awkward, as unfortunately, Norman was prone to wrath! At every opportunity, and even in normal conversation, he would see the bad in everyone and in most situations. Every slight misdemeanour or imagined mistake was greeted with some question as to the offender's parentage or sexuality, and the suitable and appropriate punishment that should be meted out to such ones was offered openly. If I had left things to Norman, I would have no male staff able to father any children or anyone with a complete set of hands!!

Nothing and nowhere was sacred to Norman. If he happened to be in the canteen and in conversation with anyone unfortunate enough to find themselves standing or sitting next to him, he would hold court, and could be heard pontificating his conclusions and judgements for all to hear. If, as an example, a member of the inspection team should, in small talk, reveal that someone had missed a part of an assembly, a dolly's eye for instance, Norman would without hesitation retort,

'And you know what I would do with them don't ya?' He would then proceed to delve into a detailed description of the punishment, causing many a listener to leave the canteen with a half eaten lunch, some with no appetite for several days afterward. He has been known on many occasions to hurl insults about anyone whom he considers 'not to be normal' (including me), although he is not always right; ....I can find my arse with both hands!

He takes particular delight in bullying the new apprentice Elves and Gnomes. There has been many a pimply youth caught out by Norman's request to go to the stores and ask our store keeper Bert for 'a long stand' or a 'left handed' spanner. One poor young Elf was seen standing outside the stores for several days running, until the penny dropped and the lad finally caught on. Later that day, Norman and Bert's locker keyholes and lunchboxes developed a strange smell of dog manure. It probably served them right! Bert has since stopped his bad habit of nail biting and nose picking and Norman has stopped licking his fingers just as he is finishing his lunch.

Norman is a large Gnome with big hands and strong, short stubby fingers, ideal for gripping spanners and the other tools used in his trade. He is a good mechanic and has kept the sleigh and flying saucers running smoothly for many years. Although he understands his job well, Norman has the opinion that without him nothing works properly and that nobody knows anything, about anything, except him. When a job is not completed to his satisfaction, Norman would fly into a rage. There have been many times a spanner or a tin of sleigh polish has been flung skywards, causing sparks to ricochet off the brick walls of the workshop.

Poor Norman, I let him down gently by explaining that the job of being my assistant required a little more finesse than he possessed, and that I already had someone in mind. Although this last part was not true, it did seem to calm him down and he returned reluctantly to his duties. Later, I quietly watched through a window and saw Norman in the workshop opening a dictionary to the letter F.

After much soul searching, another choice from

the original shortlist was invited for an interview, his name was Raymond.

The door opened and in sailed, yes sailed is the only way to describe it, a very elegant specimen. There stood before us a very tall Gnome, slightly greying at the temples and wearing his bent horn hat proudly at a jaunty angle. He wore a bright blue leather jacket, red leather trousers and sported black moleskin thigh length boots enhanced with highly polished silver buckles. A beautiful pink silk cravat completed the ensemble. I noticed almost immediately that he had the most beautifully manicured finger nails, and smelled slightly of French cologne. He sat down on one of the dried toadstools in the interview room looking a little uncomfortable.

We introduced ourselves and at our request he proceeded to outline his employment history. It turned out that during his career, Raymond had attempted a number of high profile positions. As a classically trained child actor, his 'Bottom' had been seen by many, and apparently his 'Yum Yum' was exquisitely tasteful!

After somehow contracting a throat infection, he

felt that voice projection was out of the question, and decided to seek new pastures to ply his talent. This had led him to a well known hotel in central London, England, where he worked his way from the bottom to achieve the grand status of concierge. Part of his job description was to be on hand to provide whatever services the high paying and sometimes famous clientele required. He enjoyably recalled an occasion when, late one evening, he was instructed to take a tray of drinks to an executive suite. Lightly knocking on the door, and assuming the guest would be ready for him, he entered the room, only to find two voluptuous large middle aged ladies, completely naked, about to commit serious pleasure on each other. Ever the gentleman, Raymond, without a blush, looking them both in the eye, apologised, and said 'I'm very sorry sir,' and proceeded to pour out two glasses of expensive Champagne, place the tray on a side table, and leave the room with his back to them. I could see that there was nothing stiff about Raymond. Ah, a gentleman indeed! We sat enthralled as he continued to relate his exploits.

During one hot summer, over a drink at a small tavern in London, George, a tonsorial artist friend of Raymond's, told him that he had decided to open a new salon, and asked Raymond if he would go into business with him.

The salon would cater for the modern professional person, offering up to the minute styling, shampooing, shaving, and facial massage. In the appointments lounge there was to be mood music and soft lights. The clients would be waited on by topless Goblin trainee hair artists, dressed in leather shorts and serving Pink Gin. Raymond agreed to be the manager and with his small stake injected, the new venture was opened a few weeks later to a flurry of publicity, pink balloons and show business friends During the opening first days, many a promising soap star popped in to be caught and flashed by a tipped off paparazzi.

George and Raymond had been serving the elite for about a month and all was going well. Bookings and appointments were up, and the reputation of the establishment was spreading. It was becoming quite the talk of the city.

Late one afternoon a client being seen to by a young Goblin hairdresser, requested a facial shave, an open razor shave!! The customer was a male model, the idol and well known face for a skin cream, and needed to look his best for a late night award ceremony to be held in a chic city hotel.

Open razor shaves do have a reputation for achieving a smoother and longer lasting finish than the cheaper plastic handled type purchased in supermarkets, and they are rumoured to be less painful than waxing!

Being the manager and senior hair artist, Raymond was sent for. Two or three of the other hairdressers gathered quietly around the chair, anticipating a fine demonstration of pure delight on the open razor shaving technique. Although it had been some time since he had performed an open razor shave, and not one to give up on a challenge, Raymond agreed to perform.

After first pumping the gentleman up, he settled him down to receive his requested beauty treatment. In front of his admiring audience, he proceeded to gently lower the back of the leather hairdressing chair, placing the excited client in the supine position. Hot steaming towels were placed around the models lantern like jaw and left for a few minutes to soften the stubble. The hot towels gave Raymond time to quickly open the page of an old copy of a hairdresser's manual to: 'The Open Razor: Techniques for Bloodletting and Other Business.'

Several minutes later the towels were removed and creamy shaving foam on a badger bristle brush was worked into the model's face with gentle circular movements; the relaxed customer began quietly to doze. Raymond reached into the cupboard under the shampoo basin and reverently brought out the wooden presentation case of Victorian razors that George had been keeping for just such a moment.

He paused for a while, and then selected a shiny razor, the name of the maker was beautifully engraved on the blade and it had a fine bone handle. Raymond stropped the blade on the leather belt hanging from the rear of the lowered chair, moving the blade up and down with an orchestra conductor's flourish. With the thumb of his left hand he pulled tight the skin on the model's cheek; then with theatrical poise he lifted the arm and hand holding the blade. Playing to the assembled company, he proceeded with great gusto and flair to hack at the stubble on the stars famous face.

Suddenly bursting into tears, Raymond related how the blood must have spurted at least three inches into the air, causing mass urination and fainting away by the astonished onlookers. The whole incident was made worse by the customer awakening from his slumber, and realising that his career was over, tore from the chair and began running wildly around the salon in circles, clutching his face, and spurting blood all over the floor and fittings. During the ensuing panic, Raymond quietly left the salon, elbowing his way through the gathering crowd, and pushing through the curious throng that had gathered to peer into the salon window. To the sound of an approaching wailing siren, he vowed never to return.

It was during his wanderings around the cosmic expanse to relax and forget the incident, that Raymond had spotted our advertisement in a magazine left lying around on a hall table in a cheap hotel. After applying for the post he had given up all hope of an interview, fearing that the Intergalactic police had a warrant out for his arrest.

The Tooth Fairy dried his tears and I assured him that things were going to be alright. After sending the distraught Gnome into the canteen for a square meal, the Tooth Fairy and I once again retired to my private quarters to thrash things out.

On returning to the interview office from the canteen, Raymond remarked that he had seen a large Gnome with his trousers around his ankles, apparently demonstrating using a plate, and showing some of the junior chefs what a real meat and two veg should look like. He had threatened to make something from their intestines if such a poor situation were to continue and there were no improvements to the cuisine.

'Oh, don't worry about him,' I said, 'you will eat with us on the executive table, we don't sit with the clocking in members of the staff, so the chances of having to deal with him will be scarce.' Raymond at once relaxed.

We agreed a list of duties for Raymond and

detailed a couple of Elvelets to clearing out the box room above Rudolph's stable which would now become Raymond's quarters.

Over the coming weeks Raymond proved to be a great asset to me. He expertly re-arranged the production schedules so that everything was manufactured in short batches, not one-offs as we had previously been used to. He streamlined the purchasing of materials and packaging manufacturing, and introduced new artwork to the boxes. He improved the inspection department techniques so that it had been a long time since a dolly's eye had gone missing.

The Elvelets adored him and I had noticed how over the months, their appearance had become a little more glamorous. Their face and eye make-up now co-ordinated. Their clothes, although still of Elf and Gnome design, looked a little more, haute couture, and there was always lots of excitement and furtive whispering when Raymond was about to return to work from his weekend off or his quarterly travels to Paris.

There developed a habit of kissing each other on both cheeks when Raymond handed out the little presents he had brought for them, and everybody was beginning to be called 'darling.' There certainly was an air of change about the office, but everyone seemed happy for once.

George is not a Rodney

The workshop was humming along nicely with new toys and games coming off the production line at an alarming rate, but we had noticed that wood shavings and metal swarf was beginning to make movement around the machinery awkward and dangerous. The build up was proving a little too much for the one labourer in the workshop to remove on his own without any help. Therefore it was decided on to bring in a second labourer to assist in sweeping up the floors and to make the place a little more pleasant and safe for all to work in.

As in other manufacturing operations, here at the North Pole we too have to abide by legislation that states we must employ staff from diverse educational and ethnic backgrounds, including some who would ordinarily be considered to be 'short of a shilling!'

The Intergalactic Elf and Safety at Work Act states on page 1001 paragraph 201, sub section A, Employing Loonies:

'A company shall have at least one person on its

workforce, who has poor eyesight, is hard of hearing and finds walking difficult, is basically lazy and has been recently discharged from a Government training unit.'

At our monthly production and management meeting, we concluded that we had several operators who could fit some of this description. However, our legal team was to be consulted to ensure that the factory inspector, on his annual visit, would not be minded to slap an improvement notice on the workshop if he found that we had been remiss in this area. On the evidence, and as our lawyer Mr Brown pointed out, it would be prudent that we employ a new member in the workshop who fitted the legal requirement.

I gave instructions to contact a local agency and inform them of our need for a new member of the team and waited patiently for the results of their search.

Thomas Elvin Blower, our existing labourer, was a fine gentleman. He had a short wiry body, wavy blonde locks under his bent horn hat, a lived in face and the laugh of an old pirate. He was fit for his age, keeping off the fat by cycling to work each day, amateur tap dancing on a Wednesday evening and dieting on mostly figs and Muesli; occasionally he would run. His hobby was playing the drums semi-professionally in a combo called 'The Jack Townsend Shortarse Four,' which is strange considering there were five of them.

Jack, the band leader, was a small round gnome with black, slicked, shiny brilliantined hair, parted in the middle. Thomas was on drums, Larry on the fiddle, Heric, an older Gnome, blew on a selection of empty medicine bottles and Les was an expert spoon virtuoso. The members of the band were all workers in the tool making part of the factory. In the tool room the implements which shaped the metal parts of the toys were made by hand. Then the shaping tool was attached to a machine, usually a press that formed the part to be manufactured. It was an important job to work the metal forming tools to produce a copy of itself to thousandths of an inch, and as such these Gnomes were considered highly skilled.

Heric was the tool room lathe turning expert. He

was approaching his retirement and had always been a bit of a misery even as a young Gnome. He delighted in a variety of ailments, especially after reading a medical book. His collection of empty medicine bottles became the envy of many a chemist. Laurence, or Larry as he preferred to be called, was an expert with a file and hacksaw, and could shape a square metal rod into a perfectly round bar within minutes, the filing arm movements helped him to decide to take up violin lessons.

Les was an expert machinist, he loved working the metal into the various shapes and producing the perfect working parts from a drawing. He learned to play the spoons one day whilst waiting in the canteen for the annual Nit Nurse inspection. (As you must understand, having a large amount of animals can bring its drawbacks and little visitors have been known to creep in now and then, so we keep a close eye out for any itching or infestation about our persons.)

Les had noticed when in the shower, one or two spots on his chest, and deluded himself that he had become flea infested. His nerves had built up to such a high degree that in his anxious wait to see Nursey he panicked, grabbed hold of a couple of soup spoons and began to rattle them up and down his arm trying hopefully to destroy the imagined beasts from invading his body. He found out a little later that he only had a slight heat rash but by now it was too late, his arm was black and blue and his spoon habit was fully formed.

Jack, although the bandleader, was also the foreman of the tool room, sometimes he and Thomas didn't see eye to eye, especially when Thomas was carrying out a machining role and Jack wanted the forklift truck bringing round to move some heavy object. As Thomas was the only licensed operator of the truck in the factory, he sometimes found himself in great demand, this occasionally made him a little bad tempered and at time sparks would fly between the two of them resulting in Thomas threatening to walk out or resign his post. But it always soon passed.

They decided to form the band one lunchtime when Leslie's spooning practise started them all singing in harmony; this turned into musical sessions every Friday night in Pissards Electric Saloon. Nosey

Sarah, the barmaid and landlady, imagining she would secure the band's services for free, decided to drop them in at the deep end and advertise their practise sessions to bring in more customers. When Thomas and Jack realised what was going on, they demanded a share of the bar takings. That is how their show business careers were started.

They began a successful season at 'Pissards' and were soon approached by a show business agent offering them the dance band spot with the Saucer Line of cruising flying saucers plying the outer reaches of the solar system. Sadly, they had to turn down the offer as by now the factory was entering the big production season, and it was all hands to the pump to get the toys ready for delivery. Because of their commitment at the factory, they only took on local work and parties at weekends. As their fame grew, together with a touring dog act and a bingo caller, they were elevated to play shortened sets at Town Halls throughout the North Pole, eventually becoming well known minor celebrities. Thomas once told me they numbered themselves four because early in their career, Jack would disappear into the night to the North Pole Bookies, Elfbrookes where it was rumoured he had bought shares.

Thomas would enter the workshop each morning with the cacophony of two bicycle tyre spanners being rhythmically rapped on the door; kicking it open at the last paradiddle. He then proceeded to tap and play his way along the machine beds and up the wall, finally finishing with a flourishing 'ding' on the clocking in machine set in the corner of the tool room, signalling his presence to start the day! Thomas the labourer was a happy Gnome.

The agency responded quickly to our request for a new team member and within hours had sent us George.

When I informed Raymond of the new Gnome's name he hid behind a bale of hay kept for Rudolph, until I explained to him that it wasn't the same George that he knew. This new George was a short, strange, scruffy Gnome. He refused to wear the obligatory safety blue bent horn hat, instead preferring a battered old cap that was frayed and holed, probably caused by welders sparks. He walked as though one leg were shorter than the other, lurching backwards and to the left as he moved, which transpired later to be caused by a case of piles brought on through sitting on cold metal shelves. He wore the sleeves of his dirty shirt rolled up as far as possible revealing his skeleton like arms, and held his new Government Issue sweeping brush closely to his chest. In his right ear George wore a hearing aid. No one really knew if this was real or the earpiece to a transistor radio concealed about his person, although he never failed to hear Douglas our accountant entering into the workshop on Friday pay day, carrying the workers weekly wages in his little wicker basket.

George had fascinating eyes, well not his eyes so much as his spectacles. The lenses in his spectacles reminded one of bottle ends, giving the appearance to his left eye of a dried pea, but the right one as a car headlamp.

It was quite disconcerting to catch George leaning on his broom staring at you across the workshop. He had a sickly grin, saliva dribbling from the corner of his twisted mouth. He seemed to glide almost silently from around the corner of a machine or some warehouse racking. Sometimes you knew you were in his gaze when you were caught in headlamp brightness as the afternoon light from the roof windows was reflected off George's spectacles. At this time the Elvelets seemed strangely absent.

Everyone watched George for several weeks, remarking quietly, how it was odd, that although he did move the brush in a forward manner, no dust or debris was ever seen preceding the bristles.

One day, during lunch, Thomas Elvin Blower happened to find himself on the same table as Norman our chief mechanic and stupidly dropped out in conversation what he had observed. This was grist to the mill for Norman. Up went his blood pressure, up went his arms, and up went the level of his voice.

'And you know what I would do with him don't ya?'

Then he sallied forth to explain the workings of a device that the French used to extract the life out of captured Aristocrats during the revolution, expressing to all who were in earshot that this would be the only way to deal with such a 'Rodney.'

Thomas left the canteen shaking and feeling unwell at the picture of punishment that had been painted by Norman. Unbeknown to all except an observant Elf, there in the canteen, from behind his newspaper, George had been listening.

Later that afternoon, Thomas was busily loading a wheelbarrow with the metal waste from the bicycle production line, when a maniacal scream was heard across the whole of the building. 'Yuwwwwwwww' and bang!! Metal and wooden objects began to bounce off the walls and floor around Thomas.

'I ay a Rodney!!!' Came a shout, 'Aaaaaaaagh', bang and tinkle again!

'I ay a Rodney!!'

Thomas suddenly felt the thud of a box of brass screws on his shoulder, the contents exploding and spilling all around. More throwing, including the contents of the works cat litter tray. Kat lit; cat shit, metal, wood and even his new issue government broom flew past Thomas. George had gone berserk!

He had been stalking Thomas along the inside wall of the workshop behind the storage racking and was throwing anything that came to hand at the poor drumming labourer.

'I ay a Rodney!!'

'What's a Rodney?' Thomas screamed, in fear for his life, as another object, this time a newly painted blackboard and easel found his head. The commotion was heard as far away as the medical department, whereupon the Nit nurse came running in carrying a Doctor's bag. Harold was quick to react. He appeared suddenly as if from nowhere around the workshop door wielding the biggest syringe able to be purchased from the medical catalogue 'Cadaver World.' Squealing and gurgling, Harold plunged the instrument into George, in and out the needle went with George limping and whirling first left then right trying to avoid the attack of the, by now, also mad Harold.

Moments earlier the Tooth Fairy had telephoned me to say that the Nit Nurse had seen Harold stalking George, stalking Thomas, and that Harold saw this as an opportunity to try out his new acquisition.

'I got yer,' shouted Harold.

'Dirty bastard Rodney; I got yer, haaar haaar haaar' he yelled, plunging the instrument furiously into the bedevilled George.

George's spectacles caught the afternoon light coming through the roof windows and as he spun round and around he gave the impression of a flashing headlight.

'I got yer; haaagh haaaagh,' cackled Harold even more madly than before.

'Bastard! Bastard! Bastard Rodney!!'

He was stabbing and plunging wildly with the syringe. George's skin now began to resemble a pin cushion but he refused to go down. Only later did we learn that no medicine had been drawn into the syringe, it was only filled with water. Soon it was empty.

It all ended suddenly. Norman had suspected that something was brewing. Realizing, through being tipped off by the canteen Elf, that his outburst earlier that day might have been heard by George, he had been preparing a plan of his own to dispose of the

'Rodney.' He came running out of the sleigh garage and flung himself at them, swinging the biggest spanner I had ever seen; a spanner only usually used to adjust the stroke of a pressing machine. He caught first Harold then George with a wallop to their heads. Spinning and rolling down to the workshop floor went the screaming, cackling, laughing, stabbing pair of mad men, cat excrement and saliva flying in all directions. They finally sank in a crumpled, entangled heap, gasping and sweating. Gnomes and Elves rushed to hold them down.

The Government Flying saucer was sent for. The Goblin crew, who had been here before had no difficulty in finding the workshop. With their bodies still entangled together, and spitting threats and vengeance at each other, they were bundled aboard.

(What a 'Rodney' was, no one knew, or had heard the expression before but whatever the name meant, as is usual with new expressions, it soon caught on throughout the factory and offices. It was now being used by everyone, but it had set something off in George's mind that now exploded into possible murder and mayhem.)

When things had settled down, Norman later reluctantly informed me that a 'Rodney' was a term used for a lazy bastard, but the term had not been in common use for many years. Norman had learned the expression from a strict Gnome Sergeant while in the army during his period of National Service.

He was ashamed of the outcome of his actions and assured me that his behaviour would be improving from now on. He also assured me that he hadn't meant to dispose of George, just 'smash his headlamp in' and give him a good 'kick up the arse.'

Norman, in showing off his 'superior' intellect had inadvertently reminded George of the torment he had suffered at the hands of a strict military style old Gnome foreman whom he had worked under many years before. George was slow and lazy; the foreman had compared him to his own younger brother named Rodney, who was the family black sheep. This other Rodney apparently always found ways of escaping sharing in chores around the family home, like taking out the night soil, making dung cakes for the winter fire, and turning the curing leather in the family vats. The foreman saw his brother Rodney in George and always vowed he would haunt him because of his slothful behavior. By the time the old soldier foreman was found dead in strange circumstances, George had mysteriously disappeared, only to reappear many years later at the Government Training Unit and through the agency he had now ended up working for us. In Thomas, George had now seen the reincarnation of his old adversary. He had imagined the drumming of bicycle spanners on the workshop door each morning, as the chains of hell being rattled by his old tormentor now risen from the grave and coming to get him! Because of this, George's madness had blossomed and finally flowered.

We calmed Thomas down and the Tooth Fairy offered him a rise to stay with us. He seemed pleased with this offer and the two of them went into the bicycle shed to cement the agreement.

Once the flying saucer and the Goblins in white coats had disappeared out of sight carrying their raving mad cargo, a strange eerie quiet descended on the workshop, except for the faint sound of weeping coming from somewhere in the office; it was the Nit Nurse. Only a week earlier the Nit Nurse had received news from a solicitor of a small unexpected windfall from a dead aunt. Harold suddenly had made a proposal of marriage and the future looked bright for the two of them. All her hopes were now in tatters. Poor Nit Nurse was left with only memories of what could have been.

The Tooth Fairy returned to my quarters some time later. After comforting each other, we had a stiff one and went to bed.

What an eventful day this had been!!

I had lost the North Pole doctor and wished that I hadn't followed the advice to employ George. How could I know that they were both as nutty as a fruit cake?

I hope that the Nit Nurse doesn't want a raise!

Norman, Bloody Norman!

To help the staff forget the past few days and improve morale, Raymond suggested that, as Norman had reached ten years of service with the company, a party could be held to celebrate.

It is rare that I allow alcohol into the North Pole workshops because as you have already seen, it can bring problems, but Raymond assured me that the party would make for a happy affair, so I relented.

I chaired the meeting in my office, and with me taking the minutes, I noted that Raymond, Thomas and the Tooth Fairy all enthusiastically agreed a list of duties and things to do, and together we set a date for the knees-up for a month's time.

The organisation of the party was handed to Thomas Elvin Blower. Being a musician, he had on many occasions arranged the entertainment and musical accompaniment to many a civic occasion, so this 'do,' with Thomas's contacts, should not be difficult to set up.

The Tooth Fairy had decided to call on the

services of a local Goblin male stripper as entertainment for the Elvelets, lady Gnomes and Raymond. The stripper's impression of an elephant was apparently a masterpiece known throughout the Gnome world.

Several of the apprentice mechanics began work on a percussion instrument composed of a piece of two-by-two wood inserted into an old wellington boot. Bottle tops were to be nailed into the wood to make a jingling sound as the welly would be thumped on the floor, to keep time with the band. A thumping test was carried out and with all working well, the mechanics were rightly proud of their work.

There was much excitement and preparation behind the scenes.

The party would be held in the canteen, so under the supervision of Raymond an area was cleared for the purpose of dancing and making a bandstand.

The catering was to be carried out by Mr Done, a small Goblin master baker who lived in a nearby village. He had a cheery whistle and a ready smile. He was always to be seen dressed in a brown cow-gown, with white handprints around the pockets and flour in his eyebrows and hair. The smell of newly baked bread would follow him wherever he went.

He spent a morning at the workshop taking suggestions from the staff on what their favourite treats would be, noting it all in a large blue notebook. From the mechanics there were specific requests made for ice cream, jelly, cake and pork pies. Mr Done said that he could cater for their needs, and I agreed to the order because they had all worked so hard.

The brewery chosen made real ale from the pure water of Uranus and called the golden nectar 'Pissards.' Obviously the music would be provided by 'The Jack Townsend Shortarse Four.'

Thomas was looking forward to showing off a little in front of the assembled workforce and wanted to give them a really good party. Good humour was always a strong point with Thomas, and he had cooked up a surprise ruse for the evening.

Instructing the Tooth Fairy to seek out a suitable log of wood, around fifteen inches in diameter and six inches in depth, he insisted no enquiries be made as to the purpose of the timber, but requested the use of the canteen kitchen for a couple of hours that weekend, when all the staff were sleeping, so in a mood befitting such an occasion it was agreed.

A few days later a beautiful cake made by Mr Done was delivered to the back door of the office and held in custody by the Tooth Fairy until the night of the party. The cake had ten small candles set in white icing arranged in the number 10 and was mounted on a silver base surrounded by a multi-coloured cake frill, it looked delicious.

Flags, bunting and balloons appeared as if from nowhere, and were eagerly draped across the canteen by the Gnomes and Elves, and it soon began to take on the appearance of a real ballroom.

The night of Norman's party had now arrived! The band set up early and began to play some soft music as the guests took their seats at the tables.

Earlier that day, Mr Done's freshly baked bread, cakes and treats had been delivered in large wire trays and held in my office until the evening, the smell of newly baked bread wafted into the yard outside.

In the kitchen behind the scenes there was frantic activity. The chefs toiled long and hard as the hot food was being prepared. Clouds of hot steam billowed from ovens as they were opened and chef Gordon who had been brought in for the occasion was heard above the sounds of roaring gas rings and clanking saucepans, bollocking all who got in the way of him creating.

The Goblin stripper waited to take the stage in the temporary dressing room set up for him in the kitchen, much to the disdain of chef Gordon who would have preferred the space be used for 'something more useful, rather than some silly arse with a big dick.'

The night had a magical air of excitement, I was so looking forward to the party. At precisely 7 o'clock the doors were flung open and a happy crowd surged in to take their seats at the tables.

Everyone had used the occasion to come dressed in their finery. The Gnomes and Elves wore red bent horn hats; blue leather jackets and black leather trousers, the shiny silver buckles on their shoes making them appear to be dancing on fairy dust as they walked. The ladies displayed their finest pearl necklaces and had small sparkling diamonds woven into their hair. They wore delicate lace dresses covered in shiny sequins; it was as if they were gliding on gossamer wings. The Goblins were resplendent in black tail coats, red cravats, and specially whitened spats over patent leather shoes, and they proudly carried silver walking canes

The room looked wonderful; a slowly revolving glitter ball cast little rays of light off the ceiling and walls. The bunting fluttered gently. One the white linen covered tables, candles set in wine bottles cast a soothing yellow glow. Glistening lead crystal wine glasses and gold cutlery made an impression of real grandeur.

Jack's band was on good form. As they got into the swing of the music and the evening warmed up, everyone began to relax, and the dance floor was soon filled with jigging dancers. The sounds of happy laughter and clinking glasses echoed through the factory.

Jack himself though was nowhere to be found.

Once the band had struck up, he had left quietly to check on his investments with 'Elfbrookes,' still, Thomas's paradiddles, rim shots and rhythmic mastery held the band together.

John and Doreen Eccles, the temporary bartenders supplied by 'Pissards' were busy pulling pints of the golden nectar, which was slipping down a treat. They pulled the pints so quickly that it caused some spillage, and a thin river of the liquid was beginning to flow out under the door and into the yard outside, from where some of the younger reindeers were lapping it up and beginning to giggle.

As the band played, gales of excited laughter could be heard, as different members of the audience were allowed to 'play' the welly: jingle, thump, thump, thump, thump. 'My turn now,' thump, thump, thump!

After about an hour, Raymond stepped on to the stage, waved his hand to silence the band and announced a treat for the ladies. 'Gentlemen, please make your way to the bar!' As the men moved away the ladies surged toward the stage.

'Ladies please welcome, from a successful season

at the Plastic Windmill, the Goblin King of Tease, the Buffed Buffoon, Lord of The Length,........ Pumper!!!' A great squeal arose from the Elvelets.

The Goblin appeared from behind the kitchen door and leapt on to the stage dressed as an American Naval Captain, he then proceeded to cavort about to a loud recorded version of 'Leave Your Hat On,' whilst removing a part of his garb every few minutes, much to the delight of all the ladies.

He eventually got down to a leather pouch-like affair strapped on to his nether regions by what appeared to be shoelaces; then he requested that someone in the audience join him on the stage to pour baby oil all over him. One rather chubby female Gnome, after almost being squashed in the crush, forced and elbowed her way onto the stage.

'Go on luv, anywhere you like,'

said the stripper, as he handed the baby oil bottle to the excited, sweating and gasping participant. The ladies were whooping it up,

'In the pouch, in the pouch,' they chanted.

Being a little shy, the lady Gnome began to

squeeze the oil on to the stripper's chest, and as it ran down his bronzed buffed body, the calls got even louder - 'Go for the pouch!!'

The cavorting Gnome began to make hip thrusting movements and whirl about the stage, first to the left, then the right. The witless girl, in trying for 'the pouch' missed, spilling oil in all directions. In her frenzied excitement to de-bag the buffoon, she grabbed for the shoelaces. He stepped backwards, she, already having forward motion, slipped in a pool of oil. Her head connected with his 'pouch.'

His testicles were heard cracking like monkey nuts as far away as the kitchen! 'Pumpers' eyes first bulged, then watered, then crossed, as the pain of the encounter buckled his legs and he fell to his knees. Several of the ladies moved forward offering to rub the offended testicles and make them better.

Gurgling, and unable to move, the shoelaces were snapped and his 'pouch' was torn away by the chubby girl. Her hopes of seeing the elephant were dashed; the pantless scene revealed that, rather than being 'lord of the length', with his testicles now lodged firmly in his anus, he resembled a walnut whip! Silence fell upon the crowd. The ladies began to howl that they had been cheated. Fortunately several large mechanics hauled the poor soul away in the nick of time, narrowly averting a riot. An ambulance was sent for, and poor 'Pumper' was taken to the North Pole Infirmary, sobbing along the way that his career in show business was over.

Raymond beckoned the band back on stage and as they began to play, order was slowly restored. Thump, thump, jingle, thump. The toe cap of the welly had now parted from its sole, and as it was thumped on the floor, it began to look like a gaping mouth opening and closing to the beat of the music. As the evening wore on, and the dancing became more frenzied, the welly seemed to take on a life of its own. Over the heads of the bawdy crowd we could see the welly thumping the wall. On the walls there was brass lighting with crystal glass lampshades. These proved altogether too tempting a target for the welly wielding 'Pissards' filled revellers. Thump, thump, jingle, but this time it wasn't the jingle of the bottle tops nailed to the wood that we could hear, it was the jingle of the beautiful glass lampshades being smashed to pieces. Sparkles of glass showered all over the crowd as the welly wielding louts thumped out the beat of the band on the fittings. Howls of delight could be heard above the sounds of 'The Jack Townsend Shortarse Four,' and continued until - 'Bang!' - the lights, in submission, finally fused and gave up. In the darkness the shock of the lights going out stopped the welly in its tracks. After several minutes of pandemonium, someone picked up a candle, and locating the fuse box in the kitchen, quickly repaired the fuses. The lighting came on, with still enough lamps to make the room appear romantically lit; enough to satisfy the merrymakers and tempt them back to dancing, or to their tables.

The welly was quietly removed by a public spirited Elf and hidden away in the workshop, so no more drunken destruction could be caused to any more fittings. Now, although probably much too late in the evening, Raymond again clambered onto the stage, and rattling a large spoon against a trifle dish called for order. The band cleared the stage and whilst eyes were elsewhere, Thomas quietly disappeared into the kitchen. 'Ladies and gentlemen, it gives me great pleasure ...' said Raymond, and promptly fell off the stage! The silly bugger was a little the worse for wear, but I persuaded him to rise again and continue with his presentation. Thomas reappeared grinning from ear to ear and stood behind Raymond, holding a beautifully iced cake. The Tooth Fairy was peeping from behind the kitchen door, with a look of expectation. Raymond called out for Norman to present himself on the stage.

Norman had not been in the company of Raymond before on such a formal occasion, and immediately looking him up and down, discerned by the pink Gnome outfit that something didn't quite fit the original impression that he had had of him. For a split second Norman's eyes flashed, but immediately, Raymond began to address the crowd:

'Norman has been our chief mechanic for ten years,' he swayed. 'We look forward to the next ten years and to help you celebrate; the staff would like to present you with this beautiful cake in honour of your dedicated service.' Thomas moved forward and handed it to Raymond. Norman, taken aback by the occasion and the 'Pissards,' began to sob.

'You are the nicest bunch of mates I ever had, you are the kindest celestial people I have ever met, a Gnome could never want for better friends,' large tears rolled down his cheeks. A chair was brought out of the office and a small crowd of his admirers hoisted him onto it. 'Cut the cake, Norman!' someone in the crowd shouted. A large kitchen knife was produced and carefully offered up. The photographer from 'Seasons Greetings' magazine steadied himself. Norman paused for a moment to let the flash from the camera subside and his eyesight to return to normal. With Raymond holding the cake up to him, he thrust the pointed end of the knife into the centre, as if to cut a slice. Norman's wrist felt a jolt, as the knife embedded itself into the icing covered dainty treat. The knife would not move; it could not be removed. It was stuck!! Norman pulled and pulled, eventually grabbing the knife handle with both hands and pulling wildly. The crowd descended into peals of laughter. Norman was beginning to sweat and curse under his breath. Now we know why

Thomas wanted the piece of wood! The little monster had concealed the object by covering it in icing and presenting it as a real cake. Suddenly it dawned on Norman that he had been had. 'You Bastards!' he bellowed.

He snatched the offending confectionary from Raymond and still with the knife firmly embedded, hurled it into the air.

'I might have known! You lying twisting bastards! Who is responsible for this?'

Next to the bandstand, Thomas, still grinning from ear to ear suddenly realized that Norman had spotted him. He ran through the crowd for his life. Norman swearing and cursing, leapt off the chair and began to pursue him out of the rear kitchen door and into the night. In his eagerness to bash Thomas, Norman had sprinted across the bedarkened Sleigh Park in hot pursuit of his tormentor. Unused to the exertion, a large amount of wind built up in his stomach. Almost within grabbing distance of Thomas, Norman vomited violently and slipping and slithering in his own making, fell head first into a pile of hardened reindeer manure, knocking himself out.

From out of the darkness, the sound of sirens pierced the air and headlights lit up the scene as the Intergalactic Police roared into the Sleigh Park. The villagers had reported the noise and convinced the them that someone was being shot and murdered.

I was instructed to present myself to the sergeant and had a hard time assuring him that this was a ten year party for one of our workers. We were then ordered to disperse.

After seeing the last partygoer off the premises the officers finally left, promising that if there were any more reports of a disturbance I would be arrested. Later we found John and Doreen Eccles collapsed behind the makeshift bar after finishing the last barrel of 'Pissards' whilst everyone's attention had been diverted by the fracas. Raymond decided to leave them to sleep it off and postponed the clearing up until the next day. He switched off the remaining lights and made his wobbly way to his room.

What a night!

The Tooth Fairy and I finished the real cake in my

private quarters before tucking in.

Thomas was found hiding the next day behind Rudolph's bales of hay. After assuring him that Norman was in no position to do him any harm, Raymond and I accompanied him to the medical room to confront Norman and set matters straight.

Norman lay there with a large bandage wrapped around his head with the Nit Nurse gently stroking the back of his hand.

'It will be a few days before this Gnome is fit for work,' the Nit Nurse barked at me, as I put my head around the door.

On seeing Thomas and Raymond enter the room, Norman attempted to rise, but the stars in his head caused him to immediately recline again. The Nit Nurse gave Thomas a dirty look,

'I hope you're proud of yourself!' she hissed.

After a few awkward minutes, Thomas sheepishly apologised for his trickery. Norman begrudgingly accepted, and we all agreed that it would be a long time before we did anything like this again at the North Pole.

The Nit Nurse, clucking like a mother hen, said that we had all behaved like children, and we should be ashamed of ourselves.

The next day, members of the staff were given an area of the workshop and canteen to clean and tidy, and the electrician began the task of fixing the lights. In the office we prepared to resume our normal activities and re-start production.

This night was perhaps best forgotten.

Shitzen, Santa's new reindeer

One bright crisp morning, in my post I received a letter; the envelope had a strange postmark and stamp. On opening it I read that we had been approached by a company from a large Eastern nation. It was part of their international trade delegation offering to help us with our manufacturing costs, and suggesting very competitive rates. They requested a meeting within a few days.

In the interest of Intergalactic relations, I felt that it would be nice to accept their offer of a gift. They were well known for giving presents of pandas to kings, presidents and prime ministers, but in my case they had chosen a present more appropriate, a baby reindeer. I felt that a baby reindeer would give everyone at the factory a new focus. Raymond suggested that a naming competition for our new little friend would be a good idea. The winning prize would be a makeover and Botox session in America, and a photograph taken with an 'Elfis' impersonator.

This created much excitement among the

workforce.

A few of the older Elvelets could be seen peering into hand mirrors and pulling the skin on their faces all shapes. Many of them decided to diet, anticipating being the competition winner. A cardboard box was set up by the clocking-in machine, and over the next few days a steady stream of sealed envelopes began to be deposited in it.

Early one morning Raymond despatched the communications flying saucer to the airport to collect the delegation. The Tooth Fairy made cucumber sandwiches, a large pot of tea and a selection of fairy cakes in preparation for the meeting.

'Mr. Woo, how do you do,' I said, as I welcomed the five man team of Goblins. They bowed slightly as they entered the office.

'You Missa Chrishmas Ha!'

'We bling good bisiness Ha!'

A photographer and reporter had been invited for the occasion from 'Seasons Greetings' magazine and a feature editorial had been planned for the forthcoming announcement of the anticipated trade agreement. I invited Raymond and the Tooth Fairy to be presented to the delegation and to be included in the photograph.

The leader of the party, Mr. Woo, reached into his briefcase and produced a photograph of a beautiful little reindeer lying in a bed of straw.

'This yo leindeer Missa Chrishmas,' grinned Mr. Woo, and on seeing the picture the Tooth Fairy looked as if she would melt,

'Ooh, heeths beuthiful,' she swooned.

'We post in few days Ha.'

I sat in a red leather armchair with the photograph of the reindeer on my lap, a delegate on each knee and with the others either side of the chair.

'Say cheese!' said the snapper, and off went the flash. (It was only when the photograph appeared in the magazine that we realized the flash had startled the poor visitors to the extent that they seemed to have an expression of holding back wind, their eyes almost closed, their foreheads wrinkled, and their eyebrows together and their mouths open!) With the formalities over we got down to business.

Whilst sharing sandwiches and fairy cakes and

politely sipping tea, the delegation said that they had a large quantity of different coloured paint which they could offer me at a competitive rate. Always on the lookout to improve the bottom line, I agreed an initial supply, on the understanding that I would take the rest if the colours came up to my expectations.

The Tooth Fairy had been fascinated by two of the team that kept strangely winking at her across the table. Another one was constantly grinning and the other two kept occasionally grabbing their heads.

We duly shook hands, and after an autograph session with Rudolph, Raymond escorted them back to the airport and left them waiting in the departure lounge.

On returning from his errand, Raymond suggested that a couple of the delegates were acting a little twitchy. I said that the long distance travel was the reason for the lazy eyes, head holding and tired laughter.

I instructed the Easter Bunny and Norman to make a suitable home for the new baby, and asked Thomas to clear an area of the stores in preparation for the delivery of the paint.

Several weeks later we received word that a large wooden crate was being held for us at the flying saucer freight depot. I could not remember ordering anything except the paint which was expected to be delivered directly to us, and not for another couple of weeks so I was vexed as to what it could be. Norman prepared the transporter sleigh and with me and three Elves we set off to collect the cargo.

'It's a big un, and evvy,' said the manager of the warehouse, 'I'll get someone with a forklift to shift it for you.' On the side of the crate was stencilled in large black letters 'This way up,' and, 'To boss of North Pole.' What could it be?

Eventually, the crate was loaded on to the sleigh and we set off back to the workshop, eagerly anticipating the contents.

As we swished through the thinning snow, I thought about our beautiful little reindeer, and wondered when he would be joining us, remembering that Mr. Woo promised to post him to us within a few days. I resolved to call Mr. Woo on our return.

Thomas drove the factory forklift truck around from the yard, and we unloaded the wooden box and took it into the workshop. Quite a crowd had now gathered to see what the contents were. With his voice now fully recovered, the Fire Drake honked in excitement. A large crowbar was produced by Norman and the side of the crate prized open. The side came away. There stood the fattest reindeer I had ever seen! I rushed to get my camera. In the meantime Norman, Thomas and the Nit Nurse ushered the beast into a stable next to Rudolph. When I returned to the workshop with my camera, an Elf thrust a note into my hand that he had found on the floor of the wooden crate. It was from Mr. Woo.

'Yo Missa Chrishmas, here yo leindeer, no litta ones lef, he big, bu no eat much, and paint come to you in couple of days.'

No eat much!! He looked as though he could eat us out of house and home!

I called a meeting with Raymond on how to best deal with our new arrival. Raymond, ever the clever one, suggested that we make a place for him on the sleigh harness, along with the other apprentice reindeers, and give him a good run out. It also might also be a good idea to postpone the naming ceremony until the poor lad looked more like the slim muscular winner we had hoped for, it may also avert the animal being the butt of names like 'Porker'- not what we want at all. We tore up the photograph given to us by Mr Woo as it bore no resemblance to the promised gift.

The next day a team of Elvelets was selected by Raymond to care for our new friend. After examining him, The Nit Nurse arranged a strict diet of fresh fruit, five portions, to be taken five times a day.

To begin the new exercise programme the Elves strapped the reindeer in position on the sleigh with the rest of the trainees, and a short flight around the North Pole was embarked upon. This training and fitness regime was scheduled to continue for several weeks. Apart from becoming fitter, due to the fruit diet our friend also became looser. An inordinate amount of waste was constantly plopping from the rear of the poor beast; the Elves were having quite a job keeping his stable in a fit state of habitation.

A week later a large transport flying saucer appeared over the workshop. Air traffic control had given permission for a special air corridor all the way from our Eastern supplier. It was the paint! Thomas and his team unloaded the paint and stacked it neatly in the stores. Raymond inspected the delivery. The colours were certainly vibrant if the tops of the tins were anything to go by. When Raymond informed me of this I felt that I had perhaps struck a good deal.

Before changing to the new product, we decided to test it by putting a new coat of paint on the pole at the centre of the North Pole. Seen from space, it is used to direct incoming flying saucers, and yours truly when returning from our annual excursion around the world. It has been looking a little worn and flaky for many years, so a fresh bright colour scheme was chosen.

In place of the reindeer naming competition a North Pole colour scheme competition was held instead, hastily arranged by Raymond. The lucky winner was to be drawn in the workshop on Friday lunchtime. It was well supported, although the prize this time would be a makeover by the Nit Nurse and a photo of Rudolph.

The whole of the workshop staff gathered together at lunchtime. At the stroke of midday, Raymond broke the seal on the box and invited a coy little Elvelet standing near to him to put her hand in and fish out a name.

The winner had chosen the colours red, yellow and black; no white was included because this would be difficult to see in the snow. The painting was to be carried out in the forthcoming week during the longest hours of daylight.

Norman proclaimed that he would like to lead the expedition to the pole and had decided on a team of young Gnomes to help. They had been practising with sandpaper and masking tape on the two by two wooden leg of the now disused and disgraced welly, and felt confident enough to carry out the task to complete satisfaction. I applauded their enthusiasm and said 'yes.' There was much backslapping.

Thomas helped to load the three colours of paint chosen for the project, onto the expedition sleigh. It had been decided by Raymond to give the new, as yet unnamed reindeer a chance to prove his fitness and bowel control. The new member of the family was pleased to be selected for such an auspicious duty.

To a great cheer, Norman and the other Gnomes boarded the sleigh and slipped away to paint the pole. On the journey the new reindeer plopped away quietly as the Gnomes sang a happy song. They arrived at their destination an hour later. Right away Norman organised his team and started them off by sandpapering and scraping away the old paint.

The pole itself is made of Paraná pine and stands about eight feet out of the snow. It was designed to be so tall because during a heavy fall of snow it appears to be nearly submerged. The pole could be difficult to spot from the upper atmosphere, especially if there was a snowstorm howling, so a longer pole proved to be a better navigational aid. The snow is thin at this time of the year so maximum length decoration was in order.

With a ladder placed against the pole, the Gnomes sanded and smoothed happily until Norman, running his hand over the grain, pronounced a judgement that the ideal painting surface had now been attained. A coat of quick drying primer undercoat from our own paint store was applied, and it was agreed that after lunch the real painting job would begin. The pole was now masked up to give the appearance of banding, each band would be a different colour. Norman proudly issued new paintbrushes to the team, and using a decorator's paint tin lifter, ceremonially prized the lids off the tins.

The colours really shone brightly in the sunlight. The paint had a rather strong metallic odour, but not wishing to hold up the work, Norman began painting the first band starting from the top. Each Gnome chose a paint colour and following Normans lead, began painting away. After about half an hour with Norman and his team almost finished, they began to feel dizzy, but they pressed on until the job was complete.

To save time, the half empty tins of paint were placed quickly on the sleigh, the ladder packed, and being good little Gnomes, all the used sandpaper was swept into a bag, leaving the pole area clean and tidy. They then set off to return to the workshop.

However, a rather untidy scene greeted the staff

as the sleigh rounded the corner of the works gate. All of the Gnomes were either holding their heads or laughing hysterically every few minutes, all of them had winking, twitchy eyes. The smell of the paint permeated the whole works. What could be the matter with them? I wondered. Raymond assumed immediately that they had stopped on the way back to imbibe at the tavern called 'Pissards Electric Saloon,' and like most construction workers after a good day, had relaxed a bit too much. The Nit Nurse prepared the medical room to receive the casualties. The new reindeer was unhitched and settled down in his stable by the Elvelets.

'Someone put the lids back on the paint!' I shouted, but in their haste, or having befuddled minds, they had left the lids behind at the pole. Everyone within standing distance of the lidless paint tins now also began to feel ill. It suddenly dawned; it was Thomas who shouted, 'Lead!!!' Sod it! The paint must have contained lead, an ingredient banned at the North Pole, but legal elsewhere in the world.

'Oh! What shall I do now?' I bleated.

I ran to my office and immediately rang DFEASFoG, the Department For Elf And Safety For Gnomes. A pleasant lady Gnome scientist answered the call and when I explained the problem she said, 'You have brought in illegal goods from the East, haven't you?' Oh Bugger! Now I was about to be nicked. 'Look,' she said, 'the only thing to do is to destroy the lot!'

'What about my bottom line?' I pleaded. 'You will have no bottom if you keep this stuff any longer than a couple of hours,' she spitted, 'get rid of it!!! I'm sending an inspector to you immediately!' and she slammed the telephone down.

The poor bloody Gnomes had got lead poisoning thanks to me. Now I realised why Mr. Woo and his delegation all had similar mannerisms. Thomas had by now found some old lids from our own stores and clapped them onto the offending tins. 'Fetch the communication flying saucer,' I said to Raymond and he immediately ran to the garage and brought it round to the workshop. 'Load all the paint onto it as fast as you can,' I barked! Whilst the saucer was being loaded

I rushed to the medical room.

'Norman,' I said, 'where is George?' he began to sob and laugh at the same time. With his head still hurting and his mind and brain in a fog he said, 'He is dead, I killed him, Aaaaaaahhhhhh.' 'No you didn't you silly bugger.' 'Not that George,' I assured him, 'I mean George the automatic pilot for the communications saucer.' He calmed down enough to inform me that it was the red switch located above the Pilot's seat. 'He must rest,' shouted the Nit Nurse, as I rushed out of the room.

The saucer was now loaded. There was no more imported paint left on the premises. I had to get it as far away as possible, - quickly.

'Raymond, what are the co-ordinates for the sun?' I shouted.

'What are you doing?' whimpered Raymond.

'I'm sending this rubbish to the sun. It's the only place that can completely destroy it. Quickly, Raymond, get me the numbers!!'

'You're not going to commit suicide are you boss?' he began to cry.

'Don't be so silly, I'll bale out just over the pole.'

On entering the cockpit, I punched the coordinates for the sun into the computer and fired up the magnetic motor. As I glanced through the round window over my left shoulder, I saw all the workshop staff lined up in the sleigh park, some waving hankies, others weeping openly. I strapped on a parachute, pulled down the door, and belted myself into the pilot's seat. Whoosh! Within seconds I was over the pole. I flicked the switch for 'George' and opened the escape hatch beneath my feet. Spinning and tumbling, I found myself falling to earth. On pulling the rip cord, I just caught a glimpse of the saucer heading out of the atmosphere to deliver its deadly load. I landed with a thump just a few feet away from the gleaming pole. Norman did a good job, I thought to myself, as I hastily scooped up the parachute.

Looking up I saw Raymond on the transport sleigh speedily approaching, and behind him several other smaller sleighs carrying some of the workers from the workshop, all of them were cheering wildly. I was hoisted onto the shoulders of two large Gnomes and carried back to the sleigh; this was repeated when we arrived back at the workshop, and I was triumphantly held high in front of an admiring crowd. My joy was short lived when I felt a pair of eyes burning into me. It was the inspector.

'Cum 'ere !! I wants a word with you!!'

He ushered me into my own office and immediately demanded an explanation for the state of Norman and the other Gnomes. I explained the letter from the trade delegation and Mr. Woo's offer. The inspector begrudgingly said that due to my quick thinking and bravery in disposing of the paint, that I was not under arrest at this point, but he would decide a course of action when he had consulted with his superior.

The Nit Nurse had despatched Norman and the others from our medical room to hospital. Initial reports suggested that the poisoning was only slight and that a full recovery would eventually follow after much rest. Later that evening a warrant was issued by the Intergalactic Police for the arrest of Mr. Woo and his accomplices. I realised that we now couldn't return the reindeer and that we had to choose a name for him.

The next day I decided to take the newly repaired and re-painted sleigh, the one found abandoned in the Pyrenees, out for a time trial run and put it through its paces. The sleigh was brought out of the garage and Rudolph and the others were partnered up. It was then that I thought it would be a good idea to introduce the new reindeer to the team as a little reward for his work, and the fact that he had by now lost a few pounds. Donner was asked to step aside and in his place we harnessed our new boy. With a crew of Elves on board, cracking the whip and 'Ho, Ho, Hoeing,' away we went. Oh, I do love a good Ho!

We had made excellent time and as we were returning home the gleaming finishing pole appeared in sight far in the distance. It was then that I noticed the amount of doo doo the reindeer was producing, the fruit diet was perhaps proving a little too rich for his digestive system. Just after leaving English airspace he let fly with an almighty plopper! Feeling ashamed, I ignored the outburst, and stepped up the pace to reach home. Following this excursion I had decided to call the new member of the team 'Shitzen,' after a patent medicine that I used once when I lived in the Yukon. The change in diet when I lived there bound me dreadfully but thanks to a quick thinking Dr Spearman I quickly became unbunged. I made my mind over to announce the name to all the staff at lunchtime in the canteen the next day.

Thomas proudly painted Shitzens new name above his stable. The latest recruit stood outside the door to have his photograph taken, and give an interview to a 'Seasons Greetings' magazine journalist. The new member of the team wasn't quite ready for operations just yet; shit dropping from a great height on unsuspecting people and nations was something best left to politicians, no, Shitzen would be ready to join the team when he stopped his dirty ways.

That evening in my private quarters, the Tooth Fairy and I watched the television news. The biggest solar flare ever recorded was seen by a space telescope and shown on all the news channels. Scientists were baffled as to the cause - but we know don't we? I thought it best to keep quiet.

Off the coast of Greenland several large new Islands had appeared in the sea overnight. I think I know what they could be, and I knew that they would be habitable when they went solid.

Suddenly, the Tooth Fairy produced an official looking brown envelope, it was from the Inspector. Thinking that I may as well face the music I tore the letter open. To my relief it said that 'Due to your honesty and quick thinking, we will take no further action but if you violate the Intergalactic Code of Safety again we will issue a warrant for your arrest.'

What a relief, I thought I was for or it this time!

Ah well, thank goodness that's sorted. Feeling tired and satisfied I fell asleep in front of the telly.

Fish and Fleasels

With our small communications flying saucer melted on the sun, we now had no means of quickly shipping or transporting our special orders and guests to the airport or railway station. I'd ordered another new machine from the world's largest manufacturers, B.F. Conn & Company, but due to a high demand, they could not promise delivery for at least a month. With the enforced temporary slowing down of production, we could now best utilise our time wisely by painting the workshop and oiling machinery, and generally getting everything looking spic and span.

Norman, since the altercation at his ten year party night, had lost interest in his collection of tropical fish. 'Anyway,' he said, 'they took too much looking after.' He decided to dispose of them, and placed a notice on the works bulletin board offering them for sale for the right offer. Nosey Mr Perkins, from the cleaning department, informed Norman that his son had expressed an interest in the fish. His son was a lazy and bad tempered little Gnome always getting into fights with bigger Gnomes and finding himself on the losing end. The psychiatrist had suggested that a pet would help him in curbing his aggression.

As a family always wanting a bit more than others, they thought that they would get one over on Norman and offered a price below the normal scale for the fish. They had developed a reputation among the rest of the workforce of 'skinning a gnat for his eyeball', but even though they had been told repeatedly to change their attitude, nothing worked. I suspected that one day their attempted one-upmanship would lead to serious problems. As there were several 'pets' in the tank, they felt that the effect of the 'medicine' would be more effective. They feared that the young Gnome was in danger of ruining his life and this would help him sort himself out. Knowing that the price was not fair, but having no other offers, Norman reluctantly agreed to sell the fish.

The fish were prepared for their new owner by being fed the last of the special food Norman kept in a little round pot next to the tank, and the aquarium glass was cleaned so the pets could see clearly out on the journey to their new home. Thomas had volunteered to take the fish over to Perkins' son on his bicycle after work on Friday. The new owners were to expect him around 4.30 in the afternoon.

The village of Kettle, where Perkin's son lived and let off steam, was only a short journey away, and Thomas said that he would enjoy the ride and was glad to be of assistance, and remarked that it was the only thing he could do to make amends for his behaviour towards Norman at his anniversary party.

It's our custom to have an hour put aside on Fridays to clean up the workshop, so with the way things were, Thomas was able to finish his duties a little earlier than usual. Together, he and Norman very carefully loaded the aquarium onto the wire framed pannier behind the saddle of his bicycle. Thomas went to fetch the discarded rubber bands that he had collected after the postman had scattered them on the pavement whilst delivering the mail. Several red postmen's rubber bands were wound around the glass tank and the saddle post of the bicycle. The little fish were splashing about in the tank due to the movement of the water, making the bicycle unstable, but Thomas assured us that as soon as forward motion was achieved, all would right itself. So, with Norman and Nosey Perkins watching, he flung his leg over the crossbar and with one foot on the ground and the other on a pedal, he pushed down. The forward motion of the bike caused a backward movement of the water in the tank, putting pressure on the rubber bands.

Twang!! Thunk!!

We watched helplessly as the scene appeared to unfold in slow motion. The fish tank fell backwards as Thomas pedalled off up the road. The glass shattered on the tarmac leaving the water draining away in the gutter. The helpless fish flipped and jerked in the little pile of coloured gravel and plastic toys that had graced the bottom of the tank. We were transfixed.

It had to be said that my attention was caught by the amount of noise that came from the workshop. Elves and Goblins were crying with laughter and clutching their little bellies. Thomas's face was a picture of fear, failure and dejection. The only one able to keep a straight face was the chef from the canteen; he quietly scooped the fish into a dish and carried them away.

Norman and Perkins had no other option but to walk away and carry on with their duties whilst poor Thomas sheepishly returned his bicycle to the garage. A Gnome brought out a dust pan and brush and cleared away the debris.

I later suggested an early tea, and Norman, Thomas and I made our way to the canteen. As we entered, we noticed a large 'specials' blackboard, the evening's menu was just being written:

'Special tonight, exotic fish and chips.'

In small plastic trays, set out on display along the counter, covered in a film of ice and separated into different varieties, were Normans 'pets.' Norman burst into tears and immediately turned to exit the canteen.

Earlier that summer we had promoted one of the older Gnomes to be our new labourer and part time canteen cleaner. His name was Albert. Albert had been a 'bargee' working on narrow boats on the canal system around Birmingham, England, moving coal, and occasionally pottery pieces, to London or the docks at Manchester. As he began to get older he found that the 'redeye' shifts, boating continually, taking it in turns with his other crew member to work four hours on and four hours off, were getting too much for him and he decided to come into the warm and take a job with less hours. He was a big Gnome with very large forearms and legs. His large muscles were developed from pulling, pushing and coaxing the barges, in all weathers through locks and narrow bends, and 'legging' it along the tunnels and waterways of the canal system. After mopping the canteen floor, Albert had a way of holding the stale of the mop between his palms and spinning it like an aeroplane propeller until it was dry. Many a young apprentice tried this, only to have to visit the Nit Nurse due to torn tendons in their wrists, and complaining that their sex lives were over.

Albert kept the canteen floor spotless and always put down sheets of old newspaper for us to walk on until the floor was dry. He was easily upset by any absent minded employee who happened to walk across his clean floor without wiping their shoes. It was weeping Norman who unfortunately did this, and on his sorrowful flight he carelessly walked over a part of Albert's newly cleaned but still wet floor. The galvanised mop bucket, that Albert was using, crashed on to Norman's head, spilling dirty water in all directions. Norman slipped in the water and fell backwards. As he tried to right himself, his legs were working furiously under him, but Albert was heading for him like a Spitfire attacking the Hun, his mop spinning like the Merlin engine's propeller. Norman was forcefully ejected from the canteen and into the yard, soaking wet, and, by now feeling thoroughly dejected, he stood up and walked slowly away, weeping quietly. Norman's world had collapsed around him. Unfortunately Albert kept going, spinning around the canteen seeking another 'kill,' and collided with the counter. The fish, ice, plastic containers and Albert all hit the floor together. This time there was no escape for the ex-pets. All that could be done with the melting, floppy, smelly and partly crushed remains was to feed them to the works cat. We watched the chef fold the contents into the cat's dish, leaving us feeling sorry for the afternoon's events.

One thing followed another and it was around this time that one of our little reindeers fell ill. It's rare that we have any illness at the North Pole because the temperature, being so low, kills most germs, but due to the possible effects of Global warming the last few seasons have been unusually temperate.

I was returning from a toy fair held at Pissards Electric Saloon when, on entering the works gate, I was approached by Vet Tozer. He had been summoned to the workshop stables by the Nit Nurse who had noticed several spots on one of the reindeers. Vet Tozer informed me that it was a case of the fleasles. Fleasles can be contracted by cats and reindeers when they had been rooting in the forest. It is solely a North Pole infection caused by being bitten by a small insect; the bite becomes a red blotch and is quite itchy, the patient also develops flu like symptoms.

I immediately went to the stables. Waiting for me there was the Nit Nurse and Thomas. They had been given specific instructions to keep the little chap in quarantine as a case of the fleasles was very contagious.

The reindeer had dabs of white Calamine Lotion all over his body, leaving him looking for the all the world like a Dalmatian. He smiled sadly and looked at me with big questioning eyes. 'Don't you worry, Santa will stay with you tonight,' I said, and ordered a camp bed to be made up for me in the stable.

It's quite a thing to realise just how attached one becomes to one's pets and working animals. This case was no exception. I stayed with the little chap all night dabbing his spots with Calamine Lotion and fetching glasses of water for him.

After about a week, the spots began to reduce, and the reindeer was able to sit up in bed. 'Santa,' said the patient, 'yes,' I said, 'will you tell me a story?'

I must confess that I hadn't told stories for a long time; I don't think the little reindeer meant the three greatest stories ever told: 'The cheque's in the post,' 'I will still respect you in the morning,' and 'I will always love you.' No, he wanted a little fairy story to take his mind off the fleasles. I thought for a moment, and then a story began to come to my mind that I used to tell to a little yellow haired boy many years ago when he was poorly. 'Settle down,' I said, 'close your eyes, and let me tell you about a little cat.'

'Once upon a time there was a man who had a cat, a black cat; all cats are black in stories aren't they?' The poorly reindeer nodded. This little cat always wanted to be helpful; it's good to help Dad's isn't it? 'Yes', said the poorly reindeer, 'I want to help when I'm better.' 'Well, the man decided to paint the house, and began to collect the ladders and paint to do the job.'

'What colour was the paint?' came a small voice,

'White paint for the windows,' I said.

'Can I help?' said the cat to the man.

'O.K.' said the man, 'you go and get the paintbrushes.'

The little black cat returned from the shed with a box of paintbrushes on his back and placed them at the bottom of the ladder. The man opened the paint tin and carried it to the top of the ladder, now placed against the wall next to the window. He began to paint. 'I want to help,' said his little black cat, looking up at the man.

'Climb the ladder then, but hold on tight!'

The cat climbed the ladder and stood next to the man. 'Then what did the cat do?' little voice asked. Putting the end of his tail into the paint the cat began to paint the window frame. Together as a team they brushed up and down, they finished the window in no time. It looked brand new when they had finished. But, the little cat's tail now had a white tip. 'Ah!', said my sleepy friend, and gave a big yawn. 'Look out, next time you see a black cat, see if he has a white tip to his tail. That's when you can tell if a cat helps their dad or not, if they have a white tip to their tail. Have a closer look and ask him, it just may be the cat that had been up a ladder. As a reward for being helpful the man gave the little cat some fish fingers with red sauce' All in the room was suddenly quiet. The little reindeer was fast asleep.

As is usual with these ailments, after a few days the symptoms appeared to flare up, so once again I took to my camp bed in his stable. The sad little reindeer, still spotty and glowing, looked at me with big sad eyes.

'When you are better, what would you like to

have as a present?' I asked.

'I'd like a jigsaw, a dolly in a pram, a catapult and a cowboy outfit and ....some marlies,' came the excited reply.

(Marlies, or marbles, as they should be called, are small glass balls with an inner dash of painted colour; some of them look quite exotic.)

The game is played by flicking a marble held between your thumb and forefinger and attempting to strike the other chap's marble. If you succeed then you keep the marble, quite a collection can be won in this way. 'What colour marlies would you like?' I asked.

'Well, I want some with nice patterns,' the poorly reindeer replied..

'Would you like Blue marlies, Orange marlies, Silver marlies, Sparkly marlies, Gold marlies???'..........

The little reindeer was once again in the land of Nod! A few weeks later I saw him running around the Sleigh Park with the rest of the little ones.

On seeing me he ran over and gave me the biggest sloppy kiss on the cheek. I think I will ask Rudolph to train him when he gets bigger, he is a nice little lad.

Pinkie, it's Daddy!

Norman has been distinctly quiet the last few weeks and has developed a wistful look. I think he has been feeling guilty about selling his pet fish. As you may recall he didn't get to the part of actually selling them, they ended up in the cat's tummy and I think that over the last few weeks it has been playing on his mind a little.

He has been seen by a couple of Elves drawing pictures on his locker door of his favourite fish 'pet', called Pinkie.

Apparently Pinkie was of the carp family and as his name suggests was coloured pink. Norman, whilst singing to him had taught Pinkie to follow his finger around the glass of his aquarium, they were very close. Although I confess that at times I felt that Pinkie was beginning to develop a strong hold on Norman. I caught him on a couple of occasions whilst holding his finger against the glass of the aquarium slowly opening and closing his mouth, I swear that the fish was grinning. I've never known Norman to have any deep feelings for anyone before now, but lately he has begun to express a wish to visit a well known medium one weekend to try and make contact with Pinkie to apologise for selling him.

I am getting worried about Norman. As a child many years ago he claimed to have lived in a haunted house. He said that things would go bump in the night and even the little pet dog that his parents kept was known to be nervy. It would summarily leave little shit blobs around the house, particularly at times of high wind when a ghostly whining would be heard around the ill fitting doors and windows, and a draught would become the breath of a disembodied spirit in the over imaginative mind of both Norman, and the dog! He would not believe it when a surveyor had told him that the underground railway passed directly under the house, and that this was the reason for the bumps and goings on.

At night in his bed, at the slightest rumbling, poor Norman would put his head under the bedclothes and try to be as quiet as he could, hardly daring to breath, and he would hear the muffled sound of the little dog farting and shitting in the wardrobe. This fear of the dark had remained with Norman all his life until whilst still a young Gnome, early one morning it all came to a head.

He had been out for the evening and had stayed late drinking coffee at the Mechanics Institute meeting. It was in the early hours when he returned home, and, due to the effect of the caffeine he found that he couldn't sleep. Inside the house the curtains were drawn tightly together and except for an occasional floorboard creaking all was hushed. He sat down on the old settee in the front room and decided to read a book.

After a few minutes he became aware of a presence in the room. His heart began to pound, was this in his imagination, or was he being haunted. The farting began!

As he very slowly raised his eyes from the pages of the book to look around the room he noticed that the curtains were moving. There was a presence with him in the room; Norman continued to stare at the moving curtains. With a trembling voice Norman said, 'Who is there' and the curtains began to move even more, in and out, in and out!

Finding inner strength Norman stood up, the curtains by now were flapping wildly, and so was Norman's anus!

'What do you want of me, who are you, reveal yourself' he bravely whispered.

'I've put up with you all my life now come on, what do you want'.

He walked toward the flapping curtains fully intent on wrestling with the naughty spirit. Norman raised his fists in the pose of a boxer, 'Come out and face me.'

As he moved ever closer to the imagined apparition the curtains were now moving in a rhythmical manner, suddenly Norman snatched one of the curtains open.

There behind the curtains was the little family dog, wagging his tail furiously. The little sod had taken to sleeping next to the radiator for warmth and had heard Norman enter the room.

The poor unfortunate shitter bounced twice off

the ceiling and ran yelping into the hallway and up the stairs, blobs of cac popping out in all directions. Norman stood for a while in the empty room holding his nose and trembling; he has never been the same since. It upset him so much that the next morning he visited the doctor to ask if all farts were wet! It was the memory of this experience that tipped Norman over the top and into visiting the medium.

The séance was to be held in an upper room at Pissards Electric Saloon. Around the room were several others who also wanted to speak to dead loved ones, some were just curious and came to observe, treating the whole thing as a good show and something to do on a Saturday afternoon. Nosey Sarah the landlady, greedy as ever, had advertised the event and hoped to make a few shillings out of an otherwise disused part of the establishment. Norman had arrived early and made the front row, he swore that he could smell Gin on somebody.

After a few minutes, out from behind a Chinese silk screen stepped the Medium. She was known as Madam Starlight, although her real name was Mrs

Fellatio Hawkesford, apparently her parents named her thus after taking a romantic French vacation in the 1930's. With her husband now sadly departed she lived alone in a small terraced property where she practised her art in an upstairs bedroom. The room was painted dark purple, having permanently closed curtains. She was very fond of her crystal balls and a her candles. She never had children, apparently her husband practised birth control by also having crystal balls and he could see it coming!

She was dressed for this occasion in a black cloak with silver stars painted on it and on each finger of her hands were several gold rings. Her black hair was pushed up in a beehive style and on the top she wore a knitted green fez. Her face was heavily powdered, her cheeks rouged and her red lipstick was applied in a cupid bow style almost reaching the underside of her nose. A blue smoke fug hung above the table in the dimly lit room, curling into the air from the cigarettes smoked by the nervous and expectant audience. On the table was spread a crisp white linen tablecloth, where stood a small crystal ball lit by a candle.

Suddenly the room fell into a hallowed hush.

Madam Starlight sat down heavily into her throne like armchair and off the table picked up a microphone.

'It's all right my loves, I'll just close my eyes, if I fall over just leave me, I'll be alright, I'll be alright, it's the spirit you know, it takes me like that.' She closed her eyes.

Down she went with a thump and lay there on the floor foaming at the mouth. A female member of the audience fainted, its ectoplasm, she's making ectoplasm she gasped, as her breath left her body, and she crumpled back into her seat. 'Don't be so bloody daft, she's pissed,' came a voice from the crowd. 'Somebody's coming through,' said Madam Starlight from the floor. Her voice quivered as she wiped the liquid from her mouth with the back of her hand. Madam Starlight pulled herself back on to the chair, she was a large woman and the chair looked like it would give way at any moment, so she steadied herself by leaning on the microphone stand.

I'm getting an S, someone in the room knows somebody who's gone over with the letter S.

It can't be Shortarse thought Norman, I saw him in the bookies two days ago. Just then an old Gnome lady at the back shouted, 'I know a Cyril,' 'that's it, Cyril, yes its clear now,' said Madam Starlight.

'What do you want to say to Cyril'.

'I only wanted to know how he was now, and am I forgiven?' The old lady beamed.

'Yes love, Cyril said to tell you that he never felt a thing after the first blow and he should never have complained about your cooking anyway.'

The old lady looked satisfied. Some members of the audience whispered, ...she has a gift doesn't she? nudging each other. Wonderful woman; others were heard to say!

'Now I have to speak to someone connected to a P'......'I have a strong urge for a P......'

Nobody spoke. 'I want a P' she exclaimed, at that a small youthful Gnome appeared and placed an empty plastic bucket next to Madam Starlight and giggled, 'Fill that.' He was ejected from the room and could be heard giggling all the way back to the downstairs bar.

My names Paddy shouted a little Goblin.

'Yes love it hasn't been easy has it Paddy?'

'No.'

'No love it hasn't been easy, but it's all right now isn't it?'

'Yes it's all right now'

'I know love.'

The audience clapped.

Paddy looked mystified.

The medium fell to the floor again exclaiming, 'I'm getting a floating feeling.' Norman's ears picked up.

'Oh the colours, the colours,' wailed the medium.

'Can you see any pink shouted Norman,' and stood up.

'Yes love there is.'

'It's Pinkie' cried Norman, 'Pinkie its Daddy,' he wailed.

'Pinkie says to tell you it's alright, he loves it here.'

'He's all right and having a great time'

'Are there any other pets with him,' said weeping Norman

'Oh yes love, I see lots of other cats.'

'Cats!!'

'Get him out of there,' screamed the Gnome and lunging forward violently grabbed Madam Starlight's throat.

'They will bloody kill him, get him away from them!!'

'Pinkie swim for your life!' he bawled!!

Just as her face began to turn blue several members of the audience dragged weeping Norman off Madam Starlight and held him down until the police arrived. He was carted away by two enormous Goblins and taken to spend the night in a cell at Kettle police station to cool down, and await a court appearance the next morning. The courts passed a fine and a warning that Norman should not attempt such a wicked thing again, and he must apologise and learn to strike a happy medium next time. Madam Starlight was instructed to channel her talents elsewhere. Several days later when Norman went to Mrs Hawkesford's house to take some flowers and say he was sorry, there was a note on the door.

Madam Starlight's is closed due to unforeseen circumstances.'

Put that Bloody light out!!

I had noticed of late how it was very quiet around the mechanics workshop and canteen. Norman seemed to have lost all zest for life. He spent a lot of time sitting at a table in the canteen staring into an empty tea cup attempting to see a message in the tealeaves, and swearing quietly to himself. It was pitiful to watch as an overheard comment from one of the staff about a manufacturing mistake was ignored. I remember when not so long ago Norman would descend to the depths of depravity and in no uncertain terms enunciate how best to make sure that it never happened again, but not now. I needed something to bring poor Norman back to being his old self. What could I do.

I decided to implement an idea that had been brewing in my head for a while now. I felt that we needed to project a more professional image and that perhaps a commissionaire in uniform would create the impression that we knew what we were doing. He would stand outside a newly constructed sentry box placed by the works gate. His role would be to check all visitors paperwork and on special occasions walk the important guests to my quarters and announce their presence.

Norman was asked to construct the sentry box. His countenance at once lifted and he left my office with a spring in his step that I had not seen for a while. 'What have you done,' enquired the Tooth Fairy as I explained my plan.

'It's OK it will be alright, you see!'

The mechanics shop was now closed to all visitors as Norman and his team collected wood, nails, screws and paint together to fashion his masterpiece. Within a week or so Norman requested that I appear at the door of the shop where I was to knock and await the order to 'enter.' On stepping into the workshop my eyes were immediately assaulted by a still wet bright red monstrosity of a shed bearing a sign that said, 'Stop here or be shot!'

'Oh no Norman, oh no! that is not what I had in mind!'

Norman at once flung his paintbrush into the air and kicked the can of paint spinning into the wall. On hearing the commotion Raymond ran from his office to investigate the source of the disturbance. As he charged through the door he saw the sign, he saw the red paint slowly running down the wall and pooling on the floor. Thinking that I was mortally wounded he attacked Norman with a view to seeing him off! I must confess that the workshop now resembled an abattoir with the two of them rolling about in the red paint. A couple of large Gnome mechanics pulled the pair to their feet and held them apart. I immediately ordered a cleanup, the shed dismantled and that Norman report to my office the next day.

In my office at the meeting with Raymond and Norman I sketched my idea for a sentry box. What I had in mind was the sort of box that the guards stood outside at Buck House where the Queen and the Prince of the little people lived. 'Oh, I get it now' smiled Norman, 'I thought that you wanted a border post, sorry Santa!' I arranged for Raymond to oversee the project and left them deep in discussion and went to inspect the production line. I excitedly awaited the outcome. Norman was beginning to resemble his old self again, I am pleased.

At last after several days, my presence was required in the mechanics shop to unveil the new box. It was just as I requested, resplendent in a shiny coat of grey paint, it stood tall and gave the impression of authority, without being overbearing. Raymond and Norman beamed as I sent for Thomas to collect it on the fork lift truck and place it next to the gate. A little crowd gathered to admire Norman's handiwork. The Tooth Fairy thought it was a wonderful structure and asked me what sort of person I had in mind to staff the new post. Raymond and Norman were now the toast of the works and delighted in their newly acquired fame.

I arranged to meet the Tooth Fairy in my quarters later that evening to demonstrate my thoughts on the new commissionaire and work things out with her.

The suitable applicant for the job should be an ex-military type or security guard, ideally straight backed, smart, and, because the Tooth Fairy requested it, sport a small pomaded moustache in the form of little spikes protruding each side of his upper lip.

I placed an advertisement in the 'Seasons Greeting's' magazine situations vacant column, it read; Wanted, smart military type, must be good with animals and people, preferably serious minded, having a chest full of medals and have own uniform.

From the applications we considered Dave, a security guard Elf who had been working permanent night duty at a firm that made Gnome clothing. He had been out of work for a couple of weeks after losing his job through being caught photocopying himself naked by riding on the copier platen. He thought that he had cleared everything away but the cleaner next morning wondered what a picture of a penis was doing in the waste paper basket. He claimed boredom and anyway, he said, he wanted to see himself as his girlfriend did!

Gordon was a Gnome who had been working as a bouncer at Mommercare, a well known high street chain of mother and baby outfitters. Unfortunately, due to a moment of madness, forgetting that he had once been a trainee goalkeeper, on a busy Saturday afternoon when working in a store in a small town called Titford, he was asked by an anxious pixie to hold on to a child whilst she tried on a nursing bra. The sight of the lactating beauty reminded him of lunch and glancing at his watch he realised that his break was due, just as a supervisor blew the whistle to indicate kick off for the second seating in the canteen.

The crazed Gnome, without thinking, bounced the pixie child three times on the carpeted floor and promptly toe bunted it over the cashiers glass wall. It fell into the arms of a startled cashier, none the worse for wear due to the swaddling and nappy padding. Unfortunately unbeknown to anyone, the pure in heart born again cashier had been praying to a higher intelligence and asking for a little friend to call her own. She thought that all babies came into the world this way and so for a while refused to give it back, until one of her church elders was called and helped her to see things differently! He was later caught placating her in a broom cupboard! His excuse was that he was pounding some sense into her, she was as thick as pig-shit and needed the rod of discipline! The elder was fined for being naughty and quietly removed to another congregation somewhere in England to continue his brand of teaching.

Gordon narrowly avoided prison but had to sign the dangerous gnomes act and was banned from working unsupervised for at least five years, sadly he also lost his fishing rod licence.

Although I felt sorry for him I realised that he would not really fit in as he might take to using the dollies as practise!

After much consideration we decided to invite an ex Sergeant Major Goblin named Joe Dawallock for interview. SM Dawallock had spent many years of service in the **Q**ueens **U**nder **E**ngineers and **E**lectrical **R**egiment of **S**upervisors. He joined as a boy and was pushed up the ranks until he became satisfied with his final position.

The Tooth Fairy, Raymond and me had arranged to interview him at my office.

On a sunny morning there was a sharp rap on my office door. 'Come in!' The door was flung open and in marched the candidate. 'Lef' righ', lef' righ', Sarn't major Dewallock reportin' for dooty, Sah!' and he promptly stamped his feet, saluted and came to attention before us. We looked him up and down, he was certainly a smart specimen; the Tooth Fairy was looking a little dewy eyed and Raymond was almost beginning to glow!

He wore a beautifully tailored red uniform, medal ribbons displayed on the left breast of his jacket. the silver from his lanyard and belt buckles glinted, and his shoes were so highly polished that one could see ones face reflected in the toecaps. He had the complexion of a Goblin that had spent many hours on duty outdoors and in a warm land. We invited him to sit down and take off his cap. As he did so we noticed his short haircut and the fact that he had a little pointy moustache.

At once he began to outline the reason for his unfortunate removal and early retirement from his last employ as regimental entertainments manager. He apparently had been injured when he was developing a new act for the sergeants mess, it was based on pulling his foreskin over his head and po-going between the tables on his penis to a suitable military marching tune.

He had nearly perfected the act before he almost suffocated. His request to be billed as, 'Dawallock, the controllable bollock!' was also turned down, leaving Joe very deflated. He felt that he could improve the act by po-going in a stationary position, over a mirror perhaps, rather than attempting to hop about, and he was determined to keep practising. His developing party piece was of course frowned upon by his superior officers as it was thought that he may bring the regiment into disrepute. He was though determined to make a break into show business and would think of a new act soon. He hoped that I would allow him to practise a new trick during his days off. After a brief discussion we all agreed that what he did in his spare time was his business. We decided on a three month trial for the SM and I requested Thomas to prepare quarters for him, I hoped it would all be worth it.

Within a short time, Joe was beginning to fit in well, checking visitors paperwork as they entered the yard, bringing guests to my office and saluting smartly as he left, wheeling by the left, 'quick march, lef' righ' lef' righ.' His arms pumped up and down and the sound of his shiny hob nail boots crunched on the gravel in the yard as he made his way back to the sentry box, now his pride and joy. He was a credit to us, everyone said so. On his days off he could be heard practising his party piece for the upcoming winter gathering held for all the staff and helpers, but no one was allowed to see his act, and what appeared to be the sound of rubber suckers being pulled off a glass pane could be heard from the blacksmiths shop. We all began to wonder what he could be up to.

    I had been out for the afternoon partaking in my favourite pastime of photographing reindeers, I may have mentioned this to you before, but I was by now developing quite a collection and trading them with fellow collectors around the North Pole. On my return I heard that Joe had been taken to hospital. It transpired that whilst he had been practising in the blacksmiths workshop he had become a little giddy and inadvertently slipped off his pane of glass and po-goed into a heap of smouldering coals that had been raked out of the forge as the blacksmith finished the last of the seasons reindeer shoes. I arranged to visit him at the North Pole Infirmary, he had tubes coming from everywhere. All he wanted to talk about excitedly was his new act. He said that he had the idea for a fire eating act but as usual wanted to attempt something different. He wanted to try eating the fire through his arse! Apparently the burning coals on the workshop floor had given him the idea!! I said that it was wrong to put the human body through such an experience, and anyway I had heard of this sort of thing before and I thought it was rude, but he assured me that it must be possible and was willing to give it a try. He went on to relate that he had seen a little gang of Elves drinking five star brandy behind the bike sheds and for a laugh they were having a competition as to who could light a fart and project the longest throw of flame, a sort of smelly blowlamp. I retorted that it was a silly idea, but anyway he seemed determined to pursue the idea and was keen to try it out, so until he injured himself permanently or someone else, I had to leave him to his dreams of stardom. Why do I always pick them? I left him there in the hospital bed staring into space, I think it will be a while before he is fit to work again.

Unto us a child is born

One frosty morning, Thomas approached me with something that had been brewing in his mind since summer. He had been thinking that it would be a good idea to put on our own Nativity play just before our special winter lunch. This lunch is held annually for all the staff, it's usually the last one before the big toy making push, I think I've mentioned it before, anyway, he had received the outline of a nativity play from two old pantomime directors that he had met at a garden party earlier in the year. He had been performing there with the 'Jack Townsend Shortarse Four' and had hit it off with these two old pros. The idea appeared to be a harmless one. After all, what could possibly go wrong with a nativity play? So, I gave permission to arrange for the writers to produce the play for us later on in the year.

I received a letter a few days later, informing me that choosing the players would have to begin early due to the lack of experience of the staff in these things, and the keenness of the producers to put on a good show. 'Santa, can I introduce you to the writers of the play?' said Thomas, one Saturday afternoon outside my office. Two elegant looking, but shabbily dressed Goblin gentlemen stood before me. One had grey hair, thinning slightly; the other wore a large ginger hairpiece cut in the style of a Beatles mop top, both were tall for Goblins. They were dressed in old cardigans with worn leather patches at the elbows. Their shoes were brown suede and they wore tight blue jeans held up with leather belts with large brass buckles, I noticed pink cravats under black sleeveless vests.

'Hello, dear boy,' boomed a voice.

'Santa, this is Ashford Bowdler and Samford Courtney, our writers and producers,' said Thomas.

'So glad to meet an angel,' boomed the voice, 'Sweet, sweet angel.'

It was the dulcet tones of Samford Courtney, who had been producing pantomime for the Touring Intergalactic Theatre Society for the last few years, but had now decided to start his own production company.

He put his hand on my shoulder.

'This is my partner in crime Ashford Bowdler, you may remember him from such educational films as, 'The syphilis trap,' produced for schoolchildren and 'Don't do that you will go blind,' especially made for boarding school pupils.'

'Wonderful to meet you Santa darling, love the cozzey, is it real?' said Ashford, as he gazed deeply into my eyes making me uncomfortable and a little embarrassed.

I couldn't take my eyes off the wig; it sat there like an old ginger cat asleep. I wondered what Raymond would make of all this.

'Well,' I said, 'you're in good hands with our Thomas.'

'Oh yes he truly is a pro,' they said in unison.

'I will leave it to you all, break a leg,' and I quickly disappeared into my office to meet with the Tooth Fairy and open a few letters.

Several weeks later I received a memo stating that the cast had been decided upon and could I approve the time off for rehearsals.

The play was to be entitled: 'Unto us a child is

born.'

The players were to be as follows: Joseph was to be played by Raymond. The Virgin Mary was to be played by The Tooth Fairy, I couldn't say that this was good casting but agreed none the less. The baby was a brown European Farm Girl dolly we were unable to find any packaging for. The three wise men were to be The Easter Bunny, Norman and Albert.

Some of the Elves were sent into the village to find a supplier of tea towels for their headgear. They were to play a crowd having to do obeisance to the European farm dolly. I heard later that this didn't go down well with some of them, as they all wanted starring roles in the play.

A donkey, sheep and a cow were to be real live animals lent to us by Mr Osborne, a local farmer. The star of Bethlehem would be a candle in a jam jar held high by a fishing rod wielded by Thomas.

I had to approve a large quantity of plaster of Paris, wood and hessian to make the stable and manger.

Rehearsals started to progress nicely, Saturday

mornings were set aside for the cast to run through their parts, and in the garage the set was being made by the mechanics.

An air of expectation swept the workshop. I was invited to attend the first dress rehearsal one Saturday morning at 10 o'clock sharp. They had put together a temporary stage of orange boxes with black curtains draped at the back from where, sitting on a toadstool, Thomas was preparing his 'star' and fishing rod.

From a corner of the canteen came excited chatter as the players waited for their cues to start. Some of the cast were modelling their new costumes; others were still in everyday Gnome and Elf clothes, awaiting the finishing touches from Mrs Jones the seamstress. To anyone looking on and not knowing that this was a play, they appeared to be a strange bunch. New thespians were being born.

In directors chairs, with their names stencilled across the backs, Ashford Bowdler and Samford Courtney were scanning the script. It all looked very professional.

'Quiet everyone,' said Samford clapping his

hands.

'Pacey, pacey everyone,' said Ashford, shouting through a trumpet-like affair put next to his lips, 'let's go for it, everyone to your places.'

Enter Thomas with his fishing rod, set with the jam jar candle swinging aloft on a piece of string.

'Thomas darling, stop it swinging like that there's a poppet! It's supposed to be holy.'

'I'll holy you,' said the disgruntled Thomas.

'Take it again,' Ashford said, already showing signs of agitation.

Enter Thomas again, this time walking very gingerly so as to prevent the swinging motion. The Easter Bunny, Norman and Albert were following behind.

'This looks like it,' acted Norman.'

'Oh yes, see, the star has stopped,' said the Easter Bunny. Albert in a stilted voice now began his acting career. Waving his arms and pointing to the star he said,

'We 'ave been followin' 'is star for days, this is where the King will be born, let's make camp 'ere and wait to see 'im.'

Thomas's arms were getting tired and the star began to wobble, Ashford became red in the face but said nothing. The players shuffled to one side of the stage; there was a large pregnant pause, then with everyone glancing furtively in the direction of Ashford, on to the stage came Mr Osborne, and with the help of several Elvelets the donkey and a sheep were pulled into the scene. They were arranged in a corner of the stage where eventually a manger would stand. Mr Osborne stepped forward, 'I couldn't bring the cow this mornin' as it was milkin' time an' 'er udder was full.' 'Oh get on with it,' boomed Ashford.

Mr Osborne stepped back into the shadows as Raymond swept onto the stage.

He was dressed in full costume, a sort of sacking with no sleeves, a rope belt around his middle. His Gnome hat had been replaced with a striped tea towel held on by a shoelace wrapped around his head. His shoes were of Turkish design turned up at the ends. The skin on his face had been painted with a make-up that made his face look like a small orange. All eyes were on him as he boldly stood before the cast.

'He is the new Gielgud,' whispered Samford to Ashford.

'No room at the inn, we shall stay here Mary until the child is born,' acted Raymond, his voice booming out into the empty canteen.

'Where *is* Mary?' shouted Ashford through his hailer.

'She had to go to the loo, she will be here in a jiff,' said Raymond.

'Oh bloody hell, stop!!' ranted Ashford, and with Samford Courtney's arm wrapped around his quivering shoulders, he burst into floods of tears.

'I'm surrounded by morons Samford, oh do help me,' wailed Ashford,

'Yes I know, not RADA are they?' comforted Samford.

'Everyone please take five,' said Samford.

Thomas lowered the star.

I decided to leave them to it and go back to my office. After a cup of hot chocolate, I felt an urge to visit the workshop and check on how things were progressing. The year was moving ahead apace, and the season of goodwill would soon be upon us once again.

As I entered through the door of the workshop the sounds of whirring machinery and hammer tapping greeted me. All around there were toys of every description and colour. There were pretty dolls houses, prams, red pedal cars, dollies and teddies of every sort.

The Elves had worked hard. In the corner I noticed Taf, an Elf born in the Welsh valleys, Taf was foreman over the paint spraying department and was always courteous and smiling, a friendly Elf. He was quietly staring at the palm of his hand. He looked as though he hadn't slept for days.

'Alright are you Santa? Look 'ere at what I got,' said Taf.

'What is it?'

He had a strange metal that he was swilling around the palm of his hand.

'Mercury, that's what it is,' grinned the Elf. It was then that I noticed that his gums were bleeding and that a front tooth had recently fallen out.

'Mercury! That will send you mad, where did you get it?'

'I won't tell you, well I will if you buy me a ninety niner with a flake in it,' he grinned, still staring at the liquid metal.

'Oh I love ninety niners, we 'ad 'em in the valleys you know.'

I felt that I was too late and that Taf had gone round the bend already.

'I'll be back in a minute,' I said, and promptly went for the Nit Nurse. I followed Nursey back to the workshop; she was carrying her little bag with one of Harold's syringes full of his secret medicine.

'Come on Taf,' she said softly.

'No I won't, you can't 'ave it see,' said Taf. 'I want a ninety niner with a flake, an' I want one now!'

'Where did you get it?' I asked.

'Well, I broke all the thermometers in the workshop I did, lovely isn't it?'

'Better send for the white coated Goblins Santa,' said the Nit Nurse.

At that, he dozed off for a second and Nursey

pounced and stuck the needle into the back of his hand, he fell into the arms of Morpheus. The flying saucer landed in the workshop yard, the white coated Goblins came out quietly to retrieve their sad and poor cargo. I collected the Mercury and sealed it in a glass bottle. On handing the glass bottle with its lethal contents to the senior male nurse Goblin, he gave me a stare and said that, 'I must watch it; this place was beginning to get a reputation.' They were thinking of opening a ward, and calling it The North Pole unit, I can't think why.

I returned to the canteen to check on how rehearsals were going, just in time to see the actors starting again after a lunch break. From their directors' chairs, a refreshed and composed Ashford and Samford ordered the lights of the canteen to be dimmed to 'create the right atmosphere.'

'Action!' Ashford boomed through his trumpet.

From behind the black curtains Thomas's fishing rod emerged with the jam jar lamp flickering. It moved slowly across the stage. Enter the three wise men.

'This looks like it,' projected Norman,

'Oh yes, see, the star has stopped,' said the Easter

Bunny.

Again waving his arms and pointing to the star Albert said, 'We 'ave been followin' 'is star for days, this is where the King will be born, let's make camp 'ere and wait to see 'im.'

A little quicker this time, Mr Osborne came on to the stage with his helpers, pulling the donkey and sheep and lining them up immediately at the right mark on the stage. Raymond entered, still in full stage make up and costume, this time accompanied by the Tooth Fairy who was holding a dolly wrapped in a tea towel.

'No room at the inn, we shall stay here Mary,' acted Raymond.

'Cut! What's she doing with a baby, the bloody thing hasn't been born yet!' bawled Ashford.

From behind the curtain came the gurgling chuckles of an old pirate, Thomas was losing it, the 'star' was jerking about violently.

'Oh, the tarts spoiled it,' sobbed Ashford, 'and keep that bloody star still!' he yelled.

Thomas let it all out; peals of uncontrolled

laughter rang round the canteen. The 'star' was now jerking so violently that it fell from the fishing rod, and burst on the stage. The donkey began to 'he haw' loudly, thus frightening the sheep that began to run wildly round in circles, its eyes bulging and with the Elvelets in hot pursuit. The three wise men bolted off the stage, as the flames from the candle began to lick up the black curtains. The donkey, now braying even louder, and with Mr Osborne hanging on to the reins of the beast, began to try to leave the canteen, but on doing so, in fright, couldn't help evacuating its bowels as it went.

Mr Osborne was dragged slithering across the canteen floor with donkey dung building up in the folds of his jacket. All this proved to be too much for Ashford Bowdler and Samford Courtney. They fell, weeping uncontrollably into each other's arms. As they did so, Samford Courtney's arm caught the sleeping ginger cat on Ashford's head; it slowly slid off, and as it reached the floor was caught in the flames that were now spreading rapidly. The canteen was burning down! Someone rang for the fire service, and we all went running outside to the assembly point in the Sleigh Park just as the fire engines swept into the workshop yard. We huddled together as the firemen rolled out the hoses and began to shoot water onto the flames, sending out clouds of hissing steam.

The animals were nowhere to be seen.

Mr Osborne was giving me dirty looks and had discarded his jacket.

Raymond's running eye mascara was making black lines down his orange face.

I think I'm going to retire!

Thieving little people and exploding pants

From the assembly point in the yard we watched helplessly as the flames burst through the canteen roof, sending sparks and burning embers into the evening sky. The smell of acrid smoke permeated our clothes and filled our nostrils. The fire chief did all he could to bring the blaze under control, but didn't succeed before most of the kitchen and seating area had been reduced to ashes. The last we saw of the producers was as they were sped away by a taxi sleigh to the airport, vowing never to return, or work with amateurs again!

Within the hour the insurance assessor arrived on the site. He was sympathetic but firm. He was annoyed that, for such a large factory, I had not installed a sprinkler system. I said that I certainly would in future. He jumped at me, 'You most definitely will, or we will not pay out or insure you!'

A local building firm and friends of mine, Bodgitt and Robbum tendered for the work. As no other building firm in the North Pole was capable of handling such a large project, they won the contract, and agreed to start work as soon as possible.

After many weeks of hard work and long days, the canteen had been returned to its former glory. New red plastic chairs and Formica topped tables looked very impressive in the seating area. In the kitchen, stainless steel worktops gleamed and, this time, a state of the art sprinkler and fire alarm system was installed. The smell of new paint and furniture lifted all our spirits.

I had the idea to celebrate the opening of the new canteen whilst we still had a few days left before the start of the final production schedules. As an extra treat and to add something special to the celebrations, we decided to hire a miniature railway, with open carriages drawn by a steam train, and have presents for the invited guests.

Thomas and Norman drew up a plan to have the rails laid to weave their way around the Sleigh Park and woodlands. Several plastic windmills and models of Gnomes were to be hidden at strategic points along the journey, as prizes for the ones who managed to get to them first.

The plan was to have a couple of red bearded Gnomes, Pat and Pete, who had become local legends in their own lunchtime, singing along to a guitar accompaniment, seated in the open top carriages, and as they stopped singing this would be the cue for the passengers to leave the train to forage for the prizes in the woods, a sort of musical Gnomes. Raymond was to order several fancy wooden crates of Don Perignome Champagne and a chicken in a basket meal for each of the guests.

The temporary platform and railway was installed, and just as the nights began to draw in, I set the date for the celebration. All the workers from Bodgitt and Robbum, the workshop and tool room staff and their wives were invited, along with local dignitaries, bankers and the firemen. A large marquee was erected in the Sleigh Park. To enhance the appearance of it, I had the mechanics design and build a very large chandelier. This was to be erected as the centre piece of the marquee and set above a little stage, next to a bar where glasses of Champagne would be already filled and could be picked up by the guests, along with a chicken in a basket meal.

In the early evening, guests began to arrive and were shown to the marquee by an army of Elvelets dressed in frilly French maid's uniforms with silk stockings and black suspenders, an idea of Raymond's. At first I was a little unsure of the uniforms but once I had seen the Elvelets dressed in them I gave my full approval and I swelled with pride at the wonderful sight.

As they assembled in the marquee, and while they were waiting for the engine to develop a head of steam, the guests were entertained by Pat and Pete.

I noticed that the village Mayor and a couple of bankers were grinning as the Elvelets occasionally had to bend over to serve the Champagne to those sitting down. Later on in the evening I noticed that the Mayor had a large red hand print on his face, given to him by the lady Mayor!

Pat and Pete, our red bearded entertainers, had started early on the Champagne and had snaffled at least two basket meals each before commencing their set, but they were in fine voice and rattled through their songs obviously enjoying the occasion.

After about an hour and a half the train driver approached me to say that he had got the engine ready and steamed up and ready to go. 'Get 'em aboard Santa!' the entertainers giggled, supporting an Elvelete on each arm. A happy gaggle of guests made their way to the newly installed temporary platform. They were politely seated in the open carriages by the Elvelets.

'Whooo,' went the train's whistle. Excitement rose as the little engine puffed, and to the sound of hissing steam we began our trip into the forest.

Our merry Gnomes now began to sing

'We are the Gnomes and we can help you, magic we can provide,
Sparkle in children's eyes, down on a dream you'll slide,
If you've a tear then we can change it into a happy smile,
Crying is not the style, with Santa.
In a rainbow, through a moonbeam where Santa Claus

resides,
Ice cream fountains, Sugar Mountains,
Toadstools side by side,
From dust till dawn you'll see us working,
Never to complain,
Sunny Sundays, Misty Mondays
Singing in the rain

So if you've a tear then we can change it into a happy smile,
Crying is not the style, with Santa.'

©Pete Shakespear & Pat Hannon

At the first bend on the railway track, the Gnomes stopped singing and the train shuddered to a halt. Out from the carriages and into the woods rushed the laughing throng. One large lady Gnome came back to the carriage to the cheers of her travelling companions, clutching a plastic Gnome complete with fishing rod, shouting, 'This looks like my old man!' 'Cum on,' shouted Pat, and started to strum his guitar as the train set off once again. The returning guests clamoured on to the train. Another stop, and the crowd thronged into the woods. An Elf and a well dressed Goblin banker were first to return to the train this time, each carrying a plastic windmill. Off we went again, Pat and Pete playing loudly and entertaining the passengers with their jolly song, 'Sing ya bastards!' shouted Pat and played his guitar even louder, attempting to keep the sing along going. Yet another stop, this time we had come full circle, and the finishing point was now in view.

The sight and thought of the final stop panicked the excitable merrymakers into thinking that if they hadn't captured a prize by now, they may well not do so. Without waiting for the cue to alight the train they shot from the carriages and into the forest undergrowth.

This time the trip into the surrounding trees was more urgent, and from our vantage position, sat in the carriage, we could hear the sounds of cracking plastic and raised voices. 'Let's go driver,' I yelled, 'it looks like it's getting nasty, cum on you two, play!'

As we began to slowly move off, the returnees came out of the trees; some were bloodied and began to chase after the train. 'We want a windmill!' some of them were shouting, feeling hard done to not to have found a trophy! As the train came to a halt at the platform, I fled to my private quarters.

The greedy, and by now, well oiled guests, began to ransack the woodlands and forest clearings seeking a plastic effigy of themselves or a windmill, whatever they could get their hands on. Raymond sat in the middle of the temporary platform with a bottle of Don Perignome to his lips and quaffed deeply, his tears splashing on to the wooden boards.

Pat and Pete, the red bearded Gnomes, watched helplessly as the remainder of the Champagne disappeared into the visitors vehicles. The rowdy and greedy guests began to leave the Sleigh Park carrying everything that was not screwed down. Within a few minutes what started as a good idea was all over, I felt so sad. Sometime later, when things had quietened down, there was a light tap on the office door. On opening it I saw the Tooth Fairy standing there dressed in a French maid's uniform.

'I've kept a bottle back Santa,' she whispered..............

The year has gone by really quickly so I decided to give the factory yard a fairytale air and arranged for Thomas and a couple of Elves to put out a line of candles on sticks in pretty coloured glass shades, these would form a lighted pathway from the workshop to the canteen. This little light show would, I felt, put everybody in a festive mood and encourage the final push to complete our year's production. I had instructed everybody that the candles were not to be lit until after dark whereupon we could see the full effect of the candlelight glistening off the snow, gently lighting our way.

The pace was picked up at the workshop and the warehouse began to fill up. Happy singing, hammer tapping and whistling could be heard all around the factory. At the special lunch the chef had made a beautiful meal for all the staff. Complete with party hats we all sat down in the canteen and enjoyed the feast prepared for us. I particularly enjoyed the plum pudding laced with brandy, yummy, just thinking about it now makes my mouth water! Everybody was happy, I noticed that an Elf was beginning to light the pathway of candles, and as he moved along lighting each one in turn, the light from them was beginning to sparkle on the frozen snow.

Full of well laced plum pudding and brandy, I was walking back along the lighted path to the workshop, when I stopped and bent down to tie a loose shoe lace on my slippers. Unfortunately, I felt a little wind in my tummy, and without any thought, I expelled it rather more violently than I had intended, just as the silly little Elf was lighting a candle lamp behind me. This caused an explosion that blew out the rear of my trousers and totally removed the hair on the back of my legs! It completely destroyed the lederhosen that I had taken to wearing under my costume. (This trick was taught to me by Girder, she had been taught this in Germany, and she said that on a winter's night it helped to keep in the warmth). It didn't on this occasion. Several glass lamps were destroyed either side of me. The Elf was completely shaken and distraught. I heard raucous laughter coming through the open windows of the office. My immediate thoughts were the helpers were having a good laugh at Santa again. As I entered the workshop there was a small helpless little gang standing around the office computer. Someone had logged on to the internet and they were watching a Dutch television presenter attempting a serious interview about medical procedures that had gone wrong and finding himself laughing helplessly at his guests. The assembled little gang could hardly stand up for laughing. After a few moments, I saw the funny side. I left the room quietly and without fuss, I didn't want to spoil their fun.

In my private quarters I peeled off my blackened red pants, and threw them out of the window, there was still some heat in them, and I watched a small cloud of rising steam and the snow melting where they had fallen. Now where had Girder hidden the Wintergreen? Smelling of the ointment I slipped in between the sheets of my bed and immediately fell fast asleep. They say that the Aurora borealis was seen as far South as the middle of England that night.

Girder Returns

Several weeks later as I sat in my office watching the winter light fade over the workshop, I noticed bluey green intermittent flashes appearing to come from behind the bicycle sheds. No one's welding outside at this time of night surely I thought? On stepping outside into the yard I heard clapping sounds and cheering. As I approached, a small band of Gnomes and Elves were formed in a semi-circle watching a large woman and a heavily built Gnome involved in what appeared to be a competition. They were bent over clutching cigarette lighters that were being lit between their legs, the ignition sent large sheets of flame roaring into the night air by lighting gas expelled from their backsides, it looks as though the sergeant major had started something, it must be stopped! I raised my arms and I shouted 'Stop this at once,' just as the large woman gave out a belter, but as I said it and she heard my voice she sputtered like a blow lamp as the plume of light faded. To grumbling and moaning and swearing under their breath the crowd began to disperse. It was then that I saw that the large woman was no other than Girder my old P.A.

She was annoyed that I stopped proceedings just as she was winning but was nevertheless pleased to see me. I invited her to my quarters where we could catch up on things. As she sat down on a toads tool I noticed a slight aroma of burning and another smell that seemed familiar. She had decided to visit me on her way to a new position working for some fakir in America. She was disappointed with me for letting her go, but as things turned out she had had many new adventures since leaving.

She had worked for a while as a nurse in a clinic deep in Siberia. Among other patients, she found herself nursing a particular Gnome who had appeared at the clinic with red sores on his head. She thought that it was ringworm and prescribed a cream that should clear it up, until he disclosed to her that he had found a flesh coloured rubber hat in a muddy puddle and tried it on for size. What the silly boy had contracted was syphilis off a used Johnny, daft bastard! He was so ashamed that he told the Doctor that he must have caught it off a toilet seat. The doctor said that he must have chewed it as he had also got it in his gums!

I remember something like that happened to me as a child when I contracted infantigo from rubbing heads with a reindeer. I had to have my hair shaved off and my head painted with a blue ointment. When I went to school the next day the other kids avoided me, not because of the disease, but they thought I was wearing a trainee coppers helmet!

She delighted in relating an experience about the time when two Goblins were admitted to the wards on account that they had been caught sucking lemons and were deemed to be in need of counselling, their mouths had puckered up so badly they could hardly swallow. The Portlocks were known to be a miserable pair and it showed on their faces, but it came to a head one evening in their home town in the Midlands of England.

Walter Portlock had been to the local park at dusk to walk his pet pygmy goat, when he felt a strange pressure in the air that appeared to be emanating from an invisible presence above his head. Panic set in when the goat sensed that his owner was losing it as he began to beat the air and duck up and down and was spitting foul language. The goat bolted, quickly followed by Walter. He ran all the way home, bursting into the little house sweating profusely and gasping for air. Walter was prone to panic after several times becoming detached from his bicycle when attempting a trick he saw the local youngsters use when mounting a kerb or leaping over an obstacle. The trick was performed as one rode along, rather than stop, one pulled on the handlebars and leaned back in the saddle, thereby transferring the weight to the back wheel and rising the front wheel off the ground and over the object in question. The children made this look easy and so Walter decided to attempt this whilst out on one of his cycling afternoons, and away from prying eyes. Unfortunately after getting away with it a couple of times, he tried it on the way home whilst endeavouring to mount a roadside kerb.

He landed in the front garden of a house where the unsuspecting Elf mowing the lawn heard a loud clang and a low groan just as Walter somersaulted over his hedge and plummeted to earth before him.

Not a word was said as a bruised Walter and a shocked Elf just looked at each other then Walter sheepishly let himself out by the garden gate and sloped off up the road to the sound of clanking and imprecations and 'Bloody hell, Bloody hell!' Sad to relate that he tried it a couple of days later and fell into the canal when attempting to leap over a grass tuffet in the middle of the towpath. He returned home that day leaving a trail of little canal water puddles behind him. Pond weed and grass was in his hair, and his pockets were full of tadpoles.

The panic took off big time during the park incident when he believed that he was being watched from a flying saucer and that they had indeed followed him home from the park.

The sound of buzzing and an eerie air movement around his head had firmly convinced him that they were without a shadow of a doubt attempting to capture him and abduct him to another world! He had failed to take into account that before taking out the pygmy goat he had had a bath and coated his chin all over with a new light aftershave and forgotten about the cloud of maybugs that flew in the park at this time of late evening! Attracted by the perfumed scent they must have thought that he was something to be desired and perhaps felt that they could build a nest and mate in his hair. Anyway he did eventually return home from the clinic, but vowed never to bathe again, reasoning that it was this that had made him weak. His wife had joined him in this life style and had also become panicky, refusing to allow cats in the house in case they slept across her face for the warmth and not looking into people's eyes in case she saw someone with 'a turned eye', indicating that they could be violent and prone to throwing stones at strangers.

Girder then became subdued when telling me about another patient who had booked himself into the clinic. He was a famous variety theatre performer and had been the recipient of a new experimental operation to cure a bad back. It was hoped that this procedure would make the clinic a fortune, but sadly things went wrong, that's how she lost her job.

The performer toured the English music halls with his contortion act, bending himself into impossible shapes including his pièce de résistance which came at the end of the act. It comprised of bending himself backwards and clasping his feet around a wagon wheel as it slowly revolved up into the proscenium arch as the curtains closed to the sound of the orchestra playing 'Eat more fruit.' Over the years this twisting of his body into unnatural positions had caused the bones in his back to begin to disintegrate, leaving him reduced in stature to almost four feet tall, and rendering him unable to grab onto his ankles to complete his act.

It was at a theatre called The Glasgow Empire that he suddenly heard a snapping and cracking sound and lost all feeling in his legs, and he recognised that he might have gone too far. Hence his visit to the clinic to receive his pioneering surgery.

The new technique was being developed by an oriental doctor named Furkmearder. He was using the latest material of plastic tubing in short vertebrae lengths. It was used because of its lightness and flexibility, and had metal and rubber seals enabling the tubes to slide inside each other. The apparatus was made to rise and fall and bend like the backbone. To stabilise the structure the tubes were to be filled with mercury, albeit a risky procedure but the metal was considered stable in both temperature and pressure and would hopefully conduct the electrical impulses to his muscles and nerves. After many hours in surgery a dedicated team of surgeons and nurses completely rebuilt and replaced his backbone. Furkmearder was satisfied.

The effect of the Mercury was that it acted rather like it does in a thermometer and was prone to changes in temperature, still, the team felt that the problem would settle down and after many months of recuperation and nursing from Girder our old trouper decided to leave the icy land of Siberia and take a holiday in Spain.

Girder began to weep as she continued to relate the story. As our patient was lying in the Spanish sun he fell asleep on a rubber water bed, he slept all through the midday meal and well into the afternoon.

He was found by the pool, shouting and screaming by a little waiter who did not fully understand English, but knew enough to realise that the guest who had arrived earlier that morning wrapped in blankets, and in a padded plain cardboard box, surrounded by his medical team, was not now the same height as was declared on his passport. Something was very wrong, he was now almost ten feet tall! His skin by now was red raw and stretched like catapult elastic and everyone was in fear of him bursting. His team poured water gently over his body and inserted pack ice cubes between his legs to bring down his temperature. His bathing pants were by now rent apart leaving him virtually naked on his rubber bed. He lay there being tended to, until the sun went down and the evening air cooled. It was during the night that he was quietly airlifted back to Siberia for further tests.

Girder now exploded in a cascade of tears sobbing uncontrollably. Our recovering entertainer was now staying in a recuperation chalet under the care of Girder and a landlady. The place was deep in the snowfields not far from the mountains, but it was clean and homely. The room was furnished daily with fresh flowers and he had the company of the landlady's large ginger cat that lay on the end of the bed, seemingly eyeing him up for something. After many months of bed rest exposed to the Siberian winter he finally felt able to rise from his bed On the coldest winter night on record he decided to leave his room to get himself a glass of iced water. When the landlady opened the kitchen door next morning she found only a head on the door mat and chewed plastic with rubber bits scattered around the kitchen floor. The ginger cat sat there looking quite smug, he had eaten the poor little bastard! Girder collapsed into my arms in a flood of tears, 'Oh mein fhader, it was horrible, there was mercury everyvere. The landlady said she heard a noise in der night but mistook it for somevone playing with a sqveaky toy, oh mein silly little tvister.' Poor sad Girder, I invited her to stay the night and arranged for the Tooth Fairy to have a bed made up next to mine for old time's sake.

The next morning I arranged with Raymond to let Girder see the new canteen and take a tour of the workshops to see her old friends. She was seen shaking hands with quite a few of the Elvelets until one of them invited her to a balloon dance party. This is where everyone comes to the party dressed only in strategically placed inflated balloons, something I have frowned upon since the last party where a cocky Gnome was found to have hidden a hat pin around his person with a view to using his prick to embarrass others. Within seconds her countenance changed and she began to inform the little Elvelet that she, 'had no time for joking and it vould be better for her to get back to her verk,' oh dear! I think someone may have told Girder about the incident and she didn't want a prick.

She returned to my quarters and requested to make me a curry for dinner. She had picked up the recipe on her travels to Siberia via a small island somewhere off Bangladesh. She had a couple of hours before the taxi flying saucer was expected to carry her off to the American fakir.

My quarters filled with the aromas of onions and strange spices emanating from the kitchen, my it smelled good, and she shouted through the door and asked me if I fancied a 'nan' with it, I said, 'no thank you Girder.' I thought she said did I fancy a 'man' and felt quite embarrassed at being corrected, anyway I still didn't fancy a 'nan' as I had plenty of younger talent here I could pick from, and I told her so. Girder stared daggers at me and began to throw pots and pans around creating a most awful din. I don't know what I did to upset her, perhaps she is feeling tense and apprehensive at starting a new position.

When Girder laid the table I noticed that it was only set for one. 'Have I upset you my delicate flower?' I enquired.

'No Fhader, she sighed heavily, you just thick bastard. I have to leave now, but I put food in dishes on candle food varmer for you vhen ready. I go now,' and she stepped out of the door and into the waiting taxi. Once again Girder was gone, I knew that I would miss her. Later that evening I sat down to enjoy my lonely meal so lovingly prepared for me.

In the early hours of the morning I awoke to feel a strange urge and hardly made it to the bathroom. It appeared that the curry didn't like me, and the foul stuff couldn't wait to leave my body and severely punish me on the way out. It left me at the fastest speed possible. I was helplessly exploding and emitting foul gasses, what on earth had she put into it?

I sat for hours immersed in a bath of cold water attempting to cool my poor anus that now resembled a blood orange, I could hardly stand and was experiencing partial blindness, ooh wait till I see her again! I am going to give her a jolly good seeing too!

Pissards Electric Saloon

Pissards Electric Saloon was the most popular watering hole in the North Pole. It attracted every type of person from the Intergalactic world to its fine dining, having a reputation for the best bacon sandwiches in the solar system, except when the Perkins family were in residence, they tended to hog the best sides of the pig for themselves.

It was situated a few miles out of the village; this was just as well as sometimes the noise of revelry would be carried for miles on the wind. Sarah, the landlady and resident barmaid of the establishment, was a small Gnome who, as I have already said, took an inordinate interest in other peoples' affairs.

It appeared to some, that her own private life was so boring that she made up for the shortfall by passing on any gossip that came her way. Most little people are interested in gossip, so it was easy for her to capture the ears of an audience. On a night out, it always made sense to order the 'golden nectar' from the bar, then move away to a quiet corner to enjoy it, without becoming involved in a salacious piece of information that she was only too willing to impart to an eager listener. If the person on the receiving end got to hear about the gossip, she would always blame someone else for the rumours, and you could find yourself being implicated, resulting in more than a few broken noses and black eyes over the years.

As with all such establishments, there was the 'usual characters' that could always be found propping up the bar from around five o'clock in the evening until the 'last orders' bell around eleven. One such Gnome was Coco, so called because of his large blue nose.

He could be found imbibing in the bar after work most days of the week, except Thursdays, when he had run out of money and was awaiting the 'Golden Eagle' shitting at Friday lunchtime, whereupon he would be back in the bar again that evening. There was also a small crowd of regulars who used to frequent 'the snug.' It was called this because of the log fire always burning in the grate and the fact that there was limited seating and tables, creating an intimate atmosphere. Although not having a lot of space, this room had seen its fair share of merrymaking over the years, and this night was no exception.

I heard about the disturbance at 'Pissards' the next day when Thomas called in to my office. Pulling up a toadstool he excitedly began to relay the details of the incident to me and the Tooth Fairy.

In the snug that night was a very large Goblin whose party piece was to flap the wings of an eagle tattooed on his ample chest by alternately flexing his pectoral muscles. After a few beers the Goblin, at the behest of the old ladies, would pop open the buttons of his cowboy-like shirt and perform away, cheered on by his merry friends. Late on this particular Saturday evening, whilst on his way back from the Gents, where he had deposited some used Golden Nectar; Coco inadvertently found that he had stepped into the snug. Deciding that there was a better type of crowd in the snug, and a few ladies who looked as though they may, he chose to remain there for the rest of the session.

The big Goblin was arm wrestling and bending six inch nails for a small bet or a beer. Coco watched the unfolding performance. Coco, in a fit of jealousy, could see that the big Goblin had been working out with weights since childhood and realised the puny sunken chest that he possessed was no match when it came to impressing the ladies.

The night wore on and old Coco riveted by the occasion, was spending on the Golden nectar at an alarming rate. Finally came the moment for the big lad to perform. Pop went the press studs and away he went to howls of laughter from the ladies and friends. In their merriment no one had noticed the jealous look in Coco's bloodshot eyes.

Suddenly Coco shouted loudly

'I can do that!'

'Don't be silly, have another drink and sit down son,' said the flapping Goblin.

'You think you're clever don't ya?' old Coco angrily growled, and moved to the centre of the floor.

The big Goblin, almost unable to stand through laughter, now took the cowboy shirt off altogether revealing a six pack and, to the sound of much screaming from the old ladies and cheering from the men, began to roll the muscles in his stomach in a belly dancing type circular motion. Coco exploded, and tore at his thin cardigan, ripping it off violently. Howls of laughter went up again from the crowd, the sound drawing people from the bar, and they all began to pile into the snug, compressing the already reduced space even more. Under the old cardigan was a holed and threadbare dirty vest from where Coco's belly could be seen trying to emulate the stomach movement of the trained Goblin, but instead of a rolling movement it just went in and out, drawing even more laughter.

'Aaaaaagh!' wailed Coco and grasping the vest at the neck ripped it to shreds, revealing his sunken chest and flabby old torso.

The crowd became apoplectic. (It is rumoured that through laughing so much, several elderly gnomes sustained hernias.) The crowd of old ladies lunged forward and began to claw and rip the clothes from Coco's body. Not happy just to relieve the fool of his clothes, they proceeded to throw them on the log fire and give them a poke to ensure that they burned.

They stripped the poor clown naked. His clothes, unchanged for months, exploded, his holey underpants caused a three foot gaseous flare to burst out of the fireplace, almost igniting the wind now blaring from Coco's bottom. To the sounds of what appeared to be a lunatic asylum, screaming and the most awful wind, Coco disappeared into the night and has not been seen since.

As Thomas told the story he fell off the toadstool on to the floor clutching his stomach. Poor Coco! I myself have had experience of the goings on at the Electric Saloon. Many years ago I made the acquaintance of a Gnome called Biffo.

He was labelled so because of his resemblance to a well known comic character possessing sticky out ears. He had just been granted his flying saucer licence by a judge, after losing it six months before, for driving under the influence. He and another Gnome named Harry, decided to visit 'Pissards' for a celebration drink. Biffo had arranged to collect Harry in his newly purchased sports open top flying saucer, and together they set out for the evening. The area around the watering hole was being redeveloped and several large holes had been dug to ascertain the soil composition, thereby helping the engineers to design the correct foundations for the supermarket to be built on the site. Biffo and Harry imbibed much Golden Nectar, celebrating with the other bar flies until the early hours.

On leaving the bar, the night air caught the two of them and, as they attempted to find the vehicle in the now darkened saucer park, they both began that strange walking pattern known only to those who have celebrated a little too much. Harry was feeling queasy and decided to relieve himself of a large quantity of the liquor into one of the trial pits.

He slipped in the mess and mud and ended up head first in the hole, with only his legs visible and sticking up into the air. Biffo, thinking his friend had left by another exit, managed to find his way to the driver's seat and prepared to set off home.

As he fumbled for the keys, in the darkness he heard the plaintiff cry, 'Help! Help.' A passing Elf also heard the cry and sent for the police. Biffo switched on the headlights of the saucer and caught sight of Harry's legs sticking up in the air.

'Harry don't drown!' whimpered Biffo.

'Get me out I'm covered in shit,' Harry pleaded. Biffo grabbed Harry's legs and began to pull. As Harry came up from the hole, a policeman came up in the dark to investigate. The two hapless souls half ran and half loped back to the vehicle. Biffo started the motor and Harry flung himself head first into the passenger seat. Unable to go forward due to the workings and trial holes, the saucer was rammed into reverse, just as the policeman put up his hand and shouted 'Stop!'

The policeman's foot found contact with the saucer and he went spinning like a top, over and over he tumbled, ending up in the same hole Harry had just exited from! This time Biffo lost his licence for a further three years and Harry vowed never to drink to such excess again.

The supermarket chain, decided to build its new store nearer to civilisation, and so it was never completed. The holes were eventually filled in and the area became a nature reserve complete with a pet's corner.

Crew cut Sir?

Sadly, I have just been informed by Raymond that his old hairdresser friend George has filed for bankruptcy. He has received a letter from George, asking him to help him find a job.

Poor George! It appears that all was going well until a well known Elfis Impersonator called into the salon requesting a crew cut. (He had almost been sent to jail when he had allowed Raymond to perform the open razor shave on the male model, but, due to a technicality, because Raymond, the perpetrator of the crime had disappeared, George had been allowed to remain in business.) That had been a close shave but this time things looked bad.

A junior trainee was selected to shampoo the gentleman and whilst the customers head was in the basin George prepared. George had always fancied himself as the world's best tonsorial artist and tricologist, and showed no fear when it came to furnishing the head of this show business star with his crew cut. His heart swelled with pride at the thought of the creation he was about to unveil and the reputation he would have from working on such an important and famous personality. Unfortunately, George, in his haste to finish his training and start taking money off the public, had cut short his learning, just in the week that the course instructor was outlining the 'crew cut.'

Apparently there are two types of crew cut; one type was developed for soldiers fighting in the trenches during the First World War. The style went thus: to help cut down on wound infection, all the hair was taken off the back and sides using the lowest setting on the clippers virtually up to the crown of the head, then using a special comb the top was flattened as short as possible giving the appearance of spikes.

The other style was an American version, more of a fashion statement in having a flat top left longer and a square neck finish, and leaving on the sideburns. In his grab and greed for money and fame, George had missed this. The show business star sat in the leather chair.

George ran the comb through his flowing black

locks, whilst looking at him reflected in the mirror. The hair was thick on top and thrown backwards to form a high wave and the hair at the nape of the neck was almost two inches thick. George salivated at the prospect of re-engineering the Elf's image.

'I am looking to find a lady or two tonight George,' said the Elf.

'You will be the centre of attention,' George said proudly, and began to fling a gaily patterned hairdressers gown around the customer's body. After carefully positioning a few lengths of cotton wool around the neck line of the gown, George picked up the electric clippers and set the cutting blade to number one.

Bzzzzzzzzz!!! George began at the nape of the neck, and ploughed a two inch wide furrow up to the crown of the head. The Elf's reflection in the mirror indicated that something was very wrong. His hands appeared slowly from under the gown and he began to feel the cold furrow at the back of his head. George stood back hesitantly.

'What have you done?' the Elf cried.

'You wanted a crew cut didn't you?' gasped George.

'This isn't a crew cut you pratt! I was going out to find a woman, now I will never get one.'

George sympathetically but foolishly, offered some know it all advice,

'You will,' said George, 'a bald headed one!' hoping to extract a laugh from the victim.

A young topless Goblin waiter, on seeing the embarrassment and fear on George's face, stepped in with a training manual opened to the page entitled, 'Crew-cut, variations on a style' published by 'Clippums.' Immediately George realised how foolish he had been in finishing his training too early. In his haste to show off, he had embarked on the wrong crew cut. He was performing a World War One trench crew cut, not a Hollywood star crew cut. George fainted!

One of the trainees finished the haircut as the Elf sat weeping in the chair. A completely restyled Elf left the salon to consult a solicitor and begin legal action. George was bankrupted.

Raymond was now dabbing his eyes with a large

silk handkerchief. 'Any chance Santa that we can find him a position?'

'Well, we could take him on temporarily during the build up to the winter season if he can take orders and won't be disruptive' I said.

Raymond at once began to smile, 'I will write to him straight away, I think I can use him in the packing department,' and away he skipped. I wondered what I had done.

Suddenly as I sat contemplating the last few minutes, the door to my office was flung open and there stood Norman.

'You'd better get down to the tool room quick Santa, I think they are about to start fighting!'

As we approached, Norman and I could hear Heric shouting that the rest were, 'all bastards!' What was happening? I knew that Larry could be a bit of a stirrer, but now what? Apparently, yesterday Heric had arrived for work wearing a hearing aid, the sort that looks like an earpiece for a radio. Larry insisted that the old man was not really deaf and only wanted a bit of sympathy. Instead of letting it go, he had coerced

Les and Jack, along with a couple of dim witted apprentices, to turn up for work this morning with transistor radio ear pieces in their ears posing as copycats. As they all stood in line to use the clocking in machine, Heric had taken his place in the queue and saw that they were all wearing matching devices with the wire disappearing into their jackets. He had erupted in anger, 'you bastards, you wait until you get old,' Larry you're responsible for this!' he said, waving a fist.

It took a bit of calming down but eventually Heric saw the funny side. However he still protested that he had the beginnings of oncoming deafness. I think I will arrange for the Tooth Fairy to put out a memo about horseplay. On Friday afternoon I invited the tool room boys to have a bacon sandwich with me at Pissards, I think things are all right now, but you never know.

It's been a funny year. I still think about George and the Doctor; they are both still locked up. I think about Girder and the hours she spent trying to help me relax by walking on my spine. It still hurts, and poor deluded Joe Dawollock and Taf are still not right. The

Tooth Fairy has been a good help to me this year and I think I will give her something big when I return from my round the world trip. It's about time I started getting the reindeers ready. I suppose Rudolph will start his showing off again, bloody silly animal. Oh well, it's all in a year's work, somebody has to do it! I hope you; dear reader will be good this year, you never know, I may be coming down your chimney soon. If you see a flash of light low in the Northern winter sky it's probably me on a time trial flight. I promise to cut down on the brandy. I hope to use 'Shitzen' for this year's expedition, so be careful, don't look up; you never know what he might have had to eat that day. The Tooth Fairy has asked me to say 'Hello' for her to all that I meet. I'm off for a nap now........ooh bugger, I forgot to take my wellies off before lying on the bed, where's the scraper!!

Bye for now,

**Santa and Rudolph
and all at the North Pole.**

About the author

Born in the English Midlands, Pete began to play guitar and write at the age of around fourteen. Eventually he became the only white member of a seven piece soul and reggae outfit touring the U.K. and backing many famous and popular artists of the 1960's and 1970's.

During the 1970's he went on to perform in the folk and blues clubs in England and Continental Europe. He has performed at major festivals including Germany's Osnabruck Folk and Blues festival and England's Cambridge Folk Festival leading to a successful album release 'Stay with Shakespear.'

After many years of touring Pete took a different road and entered the world of sales and sales management, holding down senior positions within several major companies in the UK.

His autobiography 'Different Roads' is now available in both Kindle and printed book form.

JH.

Printed in Poland
by Amazon Fulfillment
Poland Sp. z o.o., Wrocław